The WindSinger

PEGGY HARKINS

authorHOUSE®

AuthorHouse™
1663 Liberty Drive
Bloomington, IN 47403
www.authorhouse.com
Phone: 1-800-839-8640

First published by AuthorHouse 4/19/2011

ISBN: 978-1-4520-8020-8 (sc)
ISBN: 978-1-4520-8021-5 (dj)
ISBN: 978-1-4520-8022-2 (e)

Library of Congress Control Number: 2011906191

Printed in the United States of America

Acknowledgments:

I'd like to thank my editor for his guidance in the completion of this book. My thanks goes also to
Linda Parsons for sharing her expertise about adolescent fiction. I'm grateful to my husband Rich
for his ideas, support, and encouragement; to my son Ross and his wife Beth for their assistance on
marketing and cover design; to my daughter-in-law Tasha for her valuable feedback; and especially
to my son Richard, who tirelessly brainstormed plot ideas with me and made many suggestions
that shaped my story. Finally, I'd like to thank my grandsons, Solomon and Ethan, who helped me
"see" the young James and kept that vision alive across the months required to finish this project.

For Solomon and Ethan

Nine Years Ago

❧ ❧ ❧

CHAPTER 1

Z'Nia

Stay away from the humans.

That's what Mother would have said.

Z'Nia knew what would happen if even one of them saw her.

Mother had warned again and again: *They will track you, and they will kill you. Daughter, you must stay away from them.*

Z'Nia had always obeyed. Until today. Today, she was drawn toward danger like a honeybee to sweet nectar. From far off, she had heard the low pitch of an adult male, the higher tone of his mate, and several voices that were shrill and noisy. The humans had brought their young, and Z'Nia wanted to see them.

She moved closer, carefully planting each step on solid rock. She knew a single loose pebble could skitter down the hillside and give her away.

No one will hear me, she promised herself.

Nor would she let them see her. Her appearance would startle them, at the very least. Thick reddish-brown hair covered her body, all but her face, her hands, and her long-toed feet. And when she stretched to her full height, she could tower over most bears. Mother had once called her beautiful. But humans would not agree.

They attack out of fear, her mother had said. *And they fear anyone who looks different.*

Z'Nia felt certain the humans would fear her.

She was a Tazsmin, perhaps the last of her kind. Though she'd lived alone since her mother's death some years before, she often imagined Mother at her side. Within her mind, Z'Nia replayed their old conversations. She pretended to hear Mother's voice each morning, reminding her of work to be done. If Z'Nia needed advice, Mother offered that, too. And when the loneliness seemed almost unbearable, Mother's imagined presence eased the pain. A little.

Yet, Z'Nia sometimes felt a longing that she didn't understand. She knew only that today it drove her to spy on the humans, something her mother would never have allowed.

So when Mother's voice warned her once more to stay away, Z'Nia defiantly answered, *I can take care of myself.*

She moved in a low crouch, gliding from one shadow to the next, until she could see them. Two adults and three children. A family. Perhaps, like her, they'd wanted to be outdoors after a week of rainy days. And so they had climbed to this beautiful spot.

It was really just a meadow. In summer it would have been filled with wildflowers, though few remained this late in the autumn. The grassy field was surrounded by gentle hills that stretched upward to meet the sky. For anyone standing in the meadow, the slopes would cut off all view of the outside world. They would transform this ordinary meadow into a secret place. A private place. A hollow within the hills.

It is perfect, Z'Nia thought.

She hid among the boulders that crowned the eastern ridge. From there she could observe and listen, her back warmed by the late morning sun.

She watched with interest as the adult male led two of his young to the center of the field. He threw a round object toward them, and one of the children tried to hit it with a club.

Is it a game? Z'Nia wondered.

Long-forgotten memories crowded her mind: her mother tossing seed pods, Z'Nia chasing after them. This might be similar play, she decided.

Z'Nia saw the adult female spread a blanket, set out food, and tend to her youngest cub. Then the woman called the others to join her, and they began sharing a meal.

Z'Nia's mouth watered as the wind brought the scent of apples.

Mother and I shared apples, too, she remembered.

But apples would not satisfy the hunger she felt today. It was companionship she wanted, not food.

She remained still, her eyes darting back and forth to view the scene below. She had often watched humans from a distance but had ventured this close only once before. That time, when she was a cub herself, a young boy had seen her hiding near a forest path.

"Monkey!" he had cried.

His parents had laughed, thinking he'd made a joke.

Later, Z'Nia's mother had explained the boy's mistake. Z'Nia had laughed, too, at the notion of humans confusing the highly developed

Tazsmin with a monkey. But she also learned a lesson that day. She learned to avoid being seen.

Human cubs can be dangerous, her mother had warned.

She had explained about their sharp eyesight and curious minds. While adult humans usually ignored what they could not understand, Mother believed their children still had a sense of wonder. And like the boy on the forest path, they wouldn't hesitate to call attention to something out of the ordinary.

Z'Nia remembered her Mother's advice.

Be wary of all humans, she'd said. *And that includes their young.*

The buzz of a passing insect snapped Z'Nia's thoughts back to the present. She frowned at her carelessness.

I must remain alert, she scolded herself.

She was squatting uncomfortably behind the largest boulder on the hilltop. It concealed most but not quite all of her over-sized body. She was relieved to see neither of the adult humans looking her way. The two older children hadn't noticed her either. Unfortunately, the smallest one did.

Head cocked to one side, he stared at her boulder. His gaze traveled past it and then returned. She froze. Smiling, he looked toward his parents. As he did so, Z'Nia slid behind the rock. Surely this tiny cub would think he had imagined her.

Z'Nia could no longer see the family in the hollow below. She might have crept away. Certainly, that's what Mother would have advised. But a wave of stubbornness swept over her.

I will not leave until I am ready, she thought. *I want to know more about these humans.*

Even to herself, Z'Nia found it hard to admit her true motive. What she really wanted was to hear the playful cries that brought memories of her own childhood.

She closed her eyes, leaned back against the rock, and imagined being part of a family again. Lost in the welcome images, she soon forgot about staying alert.

And then something startled her. A low sound, not threatening in itself, but unfamiliar. Her eyes flew open. Without turning her head, she let her gaze slide to the left, then to the right. Apart from a single crow scrabbling for seeds among the rocks, nothing within her field of vision had changed.

The sound came again, a soft chuckle, much like the song of a gurgling brook.

Alarmed, she whipped her head to the side and stared into a pair of bright blue eyes. There, within touching distance, stood the smallest of the human cubs.

He laughed aloud.

Z'Nia shrank back, rigid with fright. A human had found her.

CHAPTER 2

Z'Nia

From somewhere below, a voice called out.

Z'Nia struggled to decipher a language she had previously heard only from a distance. After a moment, her brain made the necessary adjustments.

It is a command, she decided. *The child's mother wants him to come down from here.*

Part of her hoped he would obey. So far, none of the other humans had seen her. Once this child had turned his back, she could escape.

But another part of her asked, *Escape to what?*

To safety. That was Mother's voice in her head, advising her to be cautious, as always.

Z'Nia pushed the thought away. Today, she was not interested in being safe. Faced with the unique opportunity to see a human up close, she let her curiosity win out.

The child turned his gaze toward his mother, then back again to Z'Nia.

He will go now, she thought, surprised to feel dismayed.

But he didn't. Instead, he reached out to touch her.

Instinctively, Z'Nia pulled away. To be touched by a human, even one so small, was unthinkable. No Tazsmin would allow it.

Her lips peeled back, displaying teeth much sharper than her vegetarian diet required. For an instant, her blood burned with the need to strike at him.

Such a thing had never happened to her before. She gasped one hot breath, and then a second. It took a third one to stifle the snarl she felt growing deep in her throat.

What is wrong with me? she wondered. With effort, she dampened her instincts into submission.

Sharp teeth safely hidden, Z'Nia looked into the boy's eyes. She was surprised to see curiosity rather than fear, acceptance instead of distaste.

Yet we could not be more different, she thought.

6

Vaguely aware of his pale rounded face and small features, she felt mesmerized by his eyes. They were the deep blue of wild lupines, framed by dark lashes and set well apart below a smooth, flat brow. She could not look away.

In contrast, he would see- What?

Her mind called up the wavy image she had seen floating on a shallow lake. Large, dark eyes sheltered by the bony ridge of her forehead. Flat cheekbones flanking a nose that seemed slightly squashed. Skin, sun-browned and weathered to a leathery sheen.

No, we could not be more different, she thought again.

And yet he had reached out to her. She marveled at his bravery.

Z'Nia wanted to feel brave, too. For once in her life, she wanted to ignore her mother's warnings and be adventurous. Daring. Maybe even reckless.

Reminding herself that this human was far too small to pose a threat, she offered him a smile.

The boy's mother called again, "What are you doing? Come down here."

This time, Z'Nia understood the words.

The boy looked at his mother but did not answer. Then he turned his attention back to Z'Nia. He reached out again. She felt a faint shiver as she let him place his hand on her much larger one. His fingers explored the rough texture of her palm.

"Do you grow trees like my grandpa?" he whispered.

Grandpa?

Z'Nia didn't understand that word. But she did know about growing trees.

She sent a message into the boy's mind: *I care for all the earth. Not only the trees, but the flowers, the grass, and all the animals. For lakes and rivers, too, and streams. For even the smallest puddle on the beach. I care for all of these.*

His eyes widened.

Too late, she remembered that humans did not communicate with other species as the Tazsmin did. He would not have been expecting her to answer his question. Nor would he have any experience with mind-linking.

But he heard me, she realized.

The idea excited her. Could she continue the mind-link, even for a little while? What could she talk about with this tiny human cub?

He likes trees, she thought. *Perhaps he would be interested in something that comes from a tree.*

She carried a woven pouch slung across her shoulder. Now she reached inside it to find the perfectly formed pinecone she had collected that morning. She held it out to the child.

It is for you, she told him. *A gift.*

He reached for it. Then he stopped and rubbed curiously at the fine drops of rain dotting his skin. He looked up at the sky.

"James!" the mother called.

This was another word Z'Nia did not know. She decided it must be the boy's name. And she easily understood the rest of the mother's message.

"Come down here now," his mother had said. "It's starting to rain."

Over the years, Z'Nia had noticed that humans tended to avoid being outdoors during a rainstorm. She saw dark clouds mounding on the horizon. Probably, the family would leave now.

Her acute hearing brought the sound of footsteps on grass, then a scrabble of pebbles followed by a sharp cry. Pain. She concluded that the human female had been hurt.

The child paused, hand still outstretched, and glanced down into the hollow. Then he sighed and pulled his hand away.

"I'm sorry," he said. "I have to leave now."

Reluctantly, Z'Nia watched him go.

CHAPTER 3

Z'Nia

Z'Nia risked a single peek over the edge of her boulder as the child started down the path. She still hoped he might return.

But, no, the boy's mother had fallen, and the rest of the family was running to help. To Z'Nia, this represented too many humans, all of them much too close to her. No longer feeling brave, she backed away from her rock and retreated to the shelter of a birch grove a stone's throw away.

From there, she could still hear the voices, enough to know the adults were leaving and those called "Josh" and "Lindsey" would follow with their belongings. And the boy, of course. He was to go with his sister.

Disappointed, Z'Nia realized her encounter with the human cub had ended.

Her mother's voice rang inside her head. *It is for the best. What you did was incredibly foolhardy.*

Yes, Mother.

The need to defy her mother had subsided. Z'Nia closed her eyes to beg forgiveness. She imagined Mother's knowing smile.

Go home, Mother would say.

Z'Nia bowed her head. She would go.

She raised her eyes for one last look, and what she saw left her breathless with horror. The child had slipped away from his family and was now walking directly toward her birch grove, his footsteps unsteady on the hillside.

A distant clap of thunder drew the boy's gaze to the cloud-ridden sky. Distracted, he stumbled and fell headlong. She heard a *crack* as his head struck the ground. His body rolled down a rocky slope and came to rest in a low spot.

I must help him, she thought, and she hurried to his side.

Though she'd never examined a human before, Z'Nia knew the nature of living things. She saw the bloody head wound that had left him unconscious. Still, she'd known creatures to recover from injuries far worse than this one appeared to be.

He will live, she concluded.

But not unless someone found him. Already it was raining. Small streams of water drained down the hillside and pooled in the area where the child lay. In a real downpour, like those on the previous days, an unconscious person might even drown.

As this image filled her mind, the storm sent a second warning. More thunder. Closer and louder.

Z'Nia listened for human activity in the hollow. Hearing none, she believed the rest of the family had left. But she also knew how humans behaved when one of their kind went missing. Time and again, she had watched from a distance as searchers scoured the woods for a lost hiker.

They will return for him, she thought. *But if I leave him here, will they find him in time?*

She feared they would not.

Z'Nia gathered the child into her arms, intending to leave him in a safe place. But where? She pictured the family sharing their meal.

The hollow. They will look for him there.

Knowing she must hurry to avoid being seen, she headed up the incline. She paused momentarily to muster her courage before stepping into the open. That's when she heard them coming.

"James, where are you?" the father called, his voice echoed by the children's cries. "Jamesy, come out!"

Z'Nia ducked. If anyone saw her holding the boy, they would think she had attacked him. And just as her mother had warned, they would hunt her down.

And kill you, Mother's voice repeated. *Daughter, they will feel compelled to kill you!*

Terrified, Z'Nia ran back toward the birch grove. Once there, she went on running until the grove became a woods and the woods became a forest. She ran without thinking, knowing only that she must escape. Not until she reached the heart of the forest did she finally regain control of herself. Gradually, her breathing slowed, and her pace grew rhythmic. At last she stopped, panic ebbing away, and then she realized she still held the child.

In an instant, her fear returned.

Leave him! Mother's voice ordered.

Z'Nia wished she could do that. She wished she could just go on her way. But this cub was too young to fend for himself, and besides, he'd been hurt.

She thought, *I am responsible. I must care for him.*

But first she had to find shelter from the storm.

She doubled back through the forest until she reached a deep gorge cut by the river. She headed north along the top of the ravine, the river on her left. Usually, she would cross here, for she had a shelter on the other side. Though men had built no bridges in this out-of-the-way spot, she could easily ford the river on most days. Not today, though. Swollen by recent rainfall, the water gushed by at an alarming rate.

Could I swim it? she wondered. No, she decided, not with the child in her arms.

So on she went, slower now, careful of the wet earth that threatened to crumble beneath her feet. Another shelter waited at the end of the gorge. If she could get to it, she could rest and decide what to do about the human cub.

Just ahead, the ravine angled right. Z'Nia rounded the curve and stopped. She hadn't been here for over a week. The gentle waterfall she'd expected to see had become a thundering flood. Scaling the rocks near the falls would be tricky, but she felt sure she could do it once she had freed her hands.

After easing the boy to the ground, she emptied her pouch. She folded her bag around him, making sure he could breathe, and then slung it back across her shoulder. At the last minute, she retrieved the pinecone she'd offered him earlier and placed it in his hands.

Z'Nia slid one foot over the edge of the canyon and found the rough steps her mother had cut into the bank years before. She gripped the slippery rock with her strong toes and dug her sturdy fingers into whatever cracks she could find. Slowly, she made her way to a narrow ledge. Just below, the river raged against its banks.

Normally, she could easily walk along this ledge. But today, the child's weight forced her to lean into the canyon wall. She inched sideways. A little more ... and a little more. Soon, she would reach the shelter.

As the spray from the falls poured over her, she raised one arm to cradle the boy against her body. The sudden movement upset her balance. She struggled to steady herself, but her feet could find little traction on the slick rocks. Desperate, she summoned her remaining energy for just one leap.

11

Mother, help me, she prayed.

Z'Nia threw herself forward with all her might. One moment, she was flying through the air, and the next, she had plunged into icy water. But her foot touched rock. Safety. She'd taken the child to the shelter she once shared with her mother. She had taken him behind the waterfall.

Exhausted, Z'Nia stood inside her cave, facing the entrance. Only a pearly, late-day light penetrated that thunderous curtain of water. Its roar covered all sound from the outside world.

I am safe, she thought. *No one knows about this place.*

Then she looked down. A glance at the child in her arms left her chilled, as if a shadow had fallen over her. She was not safe after all.

For a moment, her panic returned. She took a deep breath.

I am a Tazsmin, she reminded herself. *I may be the last of my species. My task is to care for the earth and its creatures. All of its creatures, even this small human.*

Gradually, she grew calm. She had work to do.

CHAPTER 4
Z'Nia

Z'Nia imagined her mother's angry voice.

Daughter, what have you done? How could you have been so foolish?

The words echoed through her mind.

She blocked them out, filling her thoughts instead with details of the work she had to do. She built a fire below the smoke hole and let its blaze warm the cave. Then she wrapped the child in a blanket and laid him near the fire.

When she checked his wound, she found a bump the size of a walnut, still oozing blood. She stroked his forehead and sang a whisper-soft lullaby. As she did so, the sound of the wind rushed through the cave. Z'Nia paid no attention to it.

Her work finished, she sat down to rest at last. But now her mother's voice returned.

A human? Our enemy, here in our home? Z'Nia, how could you do this?

A sigh escaped Z'Nia's lips.

I am sorry, Mother, she replied. *I should have listened to you. I should have remembered what happened to my ancestors.*

As a child, Z'Nia had learned how the Tazsmin once lived all across the earth. In this region alone, at least five had shared the work she now did by herself. But as men invaded what was once a wilderness, they discovered the Tazsmin. Refusing her ancestors' attempts to live peacefully, men had hunted them down instead. Some of the stalkers were brown-skinned warriors with sharpened spears. Others were pale-skinned hunters whose guns roared destruction from a distance. The result was the same. The majority of the Tazsmin had been exterminated.

Worst of all, a human had killed her mother. Z'Nia would never forget that day. Horribly wounded by a hunter's bullet, Mother had dragged herself home to this cave. She lay helpless and in pain, the glow of the fire flickering across her face.

Oh, Mother, I wish I could help you, Z'Nia had cried.

The wounds were severe, and Z'Nia had not yet reached the age when her healing powers would mature.

But Mother had understood. Just before she died, she cautioned Z'Nia one last time. *Never trust a human. They will track you and kill you. Always be watchful, my daughter. Always be safe.*

Grief-stricken, Z'Nia had promised to obey. She still repeated that solemn promise each morning: *Never trust. Be watchful. Be safe.*

Today, when she'd heard the humans approaching, the memory of those warnings had driven everything else from her mind. She had been so terrified that she'd run away, not even realizing she'd taken the boy with her.

Now, Mother's voice returned, furious, accusing. It asked, *Why did you bring him here? He is our enemy.*

Z'Nia shared her mother's anger. She, too, resented the humans who had shortened her mother's life by decades.

But now she said only, *He is a child, Mother. Just a cub.*

A human cub!

But still a cub, Z'Nia said calmly.

Mother's voice became sly. *I saw your lapse, daughter.*

Centuries ago, the Tazsmin had broken away from less civilized neighboring tribes. They chose to give up hunting, fighting for territory, and the use of animals for food. Instead, they focused on caring for the earth and gradually became gifted healers.

Occasional backsliding into fierce, animal-like behavior was common among young Tazsmin of Z'Nia's age. A "lapse" of this kind signaled the transition into adulthood. Learning to focus her thoughts would help Z'Nia avoid such outbursts.

I will deal with it, Z'Nia said.

Alone? Mother challenged. *Unheard of.*

Z'Nia replied bitterly, *I do everything alone. I have no choice.*

She shut out the voice that now seemed unwelcome. Then she looked down at the innocent face of the sleeping child, noting again his smooth skin and his golden brown hair.

He is not repulsive, she thought. *And he does not fear me.*

Most humans would not have allowed the mind-link. Fewer still would have reached out to her.

Suddenly she wondered, *Could I keep him?*

She had lived alone for ten cycles of planting and harvest, more than half her life. With no other Tazsmin nearby, she had little hope of finding companionship. She would never have cubs of her own.

But what worried her most was that she would almost certainly die alone. No one would hear her last words or perform the Tazsmin burial rites as she had done for her mother. And her passing would mark the end of her species, at least in this region. After her death, who would protect the earth as she did now?

Z'Nia came to a decision. *I will keep him.*

Excited, she began planning how she could make the cave more comfortable. She would cook foods that might please the boy and weave cloth to make warm clothing for him. Most of all, she looked forward to teaching him about the history of the Tazsmin. Such a bright child should learn quickly.

A sudden movement caught her attention. The boy had awakened. He gazed at her without fear but also without love.

"Where's my mother?" he asked.

Her excitement died abruptly. She could not keep the child. He needed to be with his own kind. He needed his parents, not her.

Mother's voice returned. *You see? He does not want you.*

Z'Nia thrust the voice away and linked her mind with the boy's.

You hurt your head and were away from your family, she said. *I brought you here to keep you safe. But you will soon go home.*

She hesitated, remembering the dangers that lay outside her cave. Picturing humans who hunted without mercy, humans with guns that so easily killed, she had to force herself to finish the message.

I will take you.

He stared at her as if considering what she'd said. Then he nodded.

Z'Nia reached out toward him, pleased that he didn't pull away. She gently lifted the hair that fell across his forehead and found a large purple bruise. The bleeding had stopped, however, and the swelling had gone down.

Does it hurt? she asked.

"A little." He spoke aloud. Though he understood her mind-link, he couldn't talk to her in that way.

It will get better soon, she told him.

She hummed a bit of her lullaby. The boy looked around.

"What is that noise?" he asked.

Z'Nia knew he could hear the wind, but he would not feel its breath. Yet, she ignored his question, inviting him instead to look at her home. He put one hand on the cave's cold wall.

"Do you live here?" he asked.

Sometimes.

The boy walked around the cave. He examined her collection of seed pods and seemed delighted by an abandoned hornet's nest. He picked up an arrowhead to get a closer view, carefully running his fingers across its chiseled surfaces.

Soon he found her wall paintings. He named each symbol. "Sun ... tree ... bird ... deer."

Then he came to one he didn't know.

"What's this?" he asked.

Amused, Z'Nia saw him pointing to her self-portrait.

That is me. Z'Nia.

"I'm James," he replied. "Will you put my picture on your wall?"

Perhaps. After you have gone home.

Smiling, he wandered over to stare at the waterfall that blocked the entrance to the cave.

His eyes widened. "How will we get out?"

I know the way. We will go tomorrow.

"Good," he said. He hesitated for a moment and then asked, "Why can't you talk?"

When I speak aloud, my words are not like yours, she told him. *You would not understand. But I can use your words if I speak inside your head. Do you mind?*

"No, it's okay."

He walked around the cave some more, looking into every crack and corner.

"Where are your pets?" he asked.

Pets?

"Animals to play with. Like a puppy or a kitty."

Z'Nia frowned. Had she accepted this human cub too quickly? Why would he expect her to keep pets? The idea of treating animals with such disrespect was hateful to her.

She knew what her mother would have said. *Humans are all alike, even the young ones.*

Z'Nia felt anger bubbling within her veins. She took a deep breath to suppress it, and the emotion dropped to a manageable level.

I have no pets, she told the boy, struggling to maintain a calm tone. *Animals are not toys.*

"But you said you take care of them."

Reminding herself of his youth, she felt sure he had simply misunderstood.

I do care for them, but not as you would care for a pet. I work to keep the earth in balance. Perhaps I can show you.

"I would like to see that," he said.

His response seemed innocent enough. Z'Nia relaxed. Her anger drained away.

She prepared a supper of potatoes she'd roasted in the fire. After he had eaten, she put the child to bed. The bruise on his forehead had faded. All that remained of his wound was an angry red mark half the length of her finger.

When you wake up tomorrow, it will be healed, she said. She crooned her song again, though she knew the words, in her language, would have no meaning for him.

This time, James sang it back to her, "*Lena, sha-la loo. Nara, sha-la loo.*"

He said, "That's pretty. I like that song."

They are my words, she told him. *You would say, 'Grow in love, grow in peace.' My mother sang that song to me.*

They exchanged a smile and sang the song together while the sound of the wind flowed around them. Then James closed his eyes.

Z'Nia sat up late, watching the firelight play across his face. Again she wished that she could keep him, but that was impossible.

How will I get him home? she wondered.

Humans would be out looking for him. Would they be looking for her, too? Would they have guns? She tensed at the thought. Then she realized only James had seen her. Still, taking him home meant going into human territory, a frightening prospect.

What should I do, Mother? she asked.

But the voice that so often haunted her thoughts now remained stubbornly silent.

Left on her own to puzzle out a solution to her problem, Z'Nia at last decided, *Perhaps I can leave him where one of the searchers will find him.*

That might work. But with humans combing the forest for any sign of James, she'd still have to avoid being seen. She'd made a big mistake today. The next one could be her last.

She inspected the boy's wound one more time and found only a faint red line. Though she had never healed a human before, she felt confident she could erase even that last trace of his injury. She touched his head, feeling the warmth of her power pulsing through her fingertips.

Grow in love, James, she whispered. *Grow in peace.*

She hummed softly, and her song became the wind. It swelled until it filled the cave, wrapping Z'Nia and the boy in its melody.

She rested her weary head against one hand, for the act of healing the boy had sapped her energy. But she never stopped watching that faint red line. It faded, faded, and then it disappeared altogether.

You will be sorry, her mother warned.

But the wind carried her voice away. And the cave was silent.

CHAPTER 5
Z'Nia

Z'Nia woke early and saw the river settling back to its normal level. She packed food, her perfect pinecone, and an arrowhead James had admired. While he slept, she ducked through the falls and climbed to the top of the gorge. She unloaded her supplies, then returned to get the boy. James didn't stir when she folded her pouch around him. Even the climb up the banks left him undisturbed.

No longer needing both hands for climbing, she picked up her supplies and set off. Her long, loping strides soon took her far from the waterfall. When she'd covered enough distance that James could never find the way back, she nudged him awake.

His eyes opened.

"We're out," he said.

Yes, we are going to find your family.

Z'Nia set him down and gave him some food. The boy smiled when he saw the pinecone and arrowhead.

I brought them for you, she said.

While James ate breakfast, Z'Nia examined the plants covering the forest floor. She fingered a drooping fern and whispered a song that was soft as a gentle breeze. The fern straightened. Its leaves furled outward, greener than before.

She moved from plant to plant, singing her song of healing and hope. She sang to the field mice and the deer, to the tiniest ants and the tallest trees.

A solitary crow settled onto a nearby branch. Aloof, it looked away from Z'Nia and preened its glossy feathers. She sang to it. The dark, glittering eyes turned toward her. She sang again, and the bird answered. *Caw.*

Another black bird joined the first. Now four bright eyes stared at Z'Nia.

Suddenly, she heard a voice.

"*Sha-la loo,*" James sang to a cricket. "Grow in love. Grow in peace."

The cricket chirped in return.

As always, the healing lifted Z'Nia's spirit.

You sing very well, she said.

"It's my song. You gave it to me last night."

Yes, I did. Now you see how I care for all living things.

"Can I help?"

You already have.

Soon, they had to move on. Noticing the crows were following them, she cautioned James to stay quiet.

"Can I whisper?" he asked.

Yes, but very softly.

From time to time, he asked questions. Z'Nia helped him identify trees and explained how birds built their nests. She was showing him a cocoon when she heard a human voice. Normally, she would have run into the forest. But today, she hesitated. She needed to know if she could trust this person.

No more talking, she said. *A human is nearby. It may be a good person who will take you home. Or it may not. We will find out.*

Eyes wide, James allowed her to carry him.

Z'Nia crept across the paths. Her excellent hearing told her exactly where to find the owner of this voice. Soon, she heard a second voice. She listened intently to their conversation.

Guns! They had guns!

Frightened, she moved deeper among the trees until she reached the most secret part of the forest. But even there, surrounded by the woodland she loved, fear stole her breath away.

James stared up at her. "Were they bad people?"

They have guns, she said. *They might hurt the animals. Or me.*

He wrapped his arms around her neck.

"I won't let them hurt you," he replied.

Z'Nia hesitated and then hugged him back. James would be with her for one more day. She felt joyful but guilty, too.

I am sorry, she said. *We will try again tomorrow. I promise we will find the right person to take you home.*

Not wanting to return to the cave behind the waterfall, Z'Nia took him to another of her shelters. He slept soundly through the night, though she remained alert. For what, she didn't know.

The next morning, she chose a roundabout route to the hillside where she'd first seen James. On the way, she pointed out vines that could be braided into rope and helped him make a six-foot length. She showed him how to use a fallen log to cross a stream.

Suddenly James pointed at something that lay on the ground. "Oh, no. Look!"

Z'Nia found an injured sparrow, still warm but scarcely breathing. She picked it up. Half a dozen crows flew over to watch as she examined it.

She wondered at their attention. *Do they not trust me to care for this bird? I must prove to them I mean no harm.*

Seeing the sparrow had broken its left wing, she stroked its feathers until they looked almost perfect. All the while she sang, and the sound of the wind swirled around them. At last, the bird opened its eyes and breathed normally. Z'Nia sent it soaring into the sky.

She watched it for a long time and then sat for a little while to regain her strength. The crows came nearer. The boldest of them even perched on her shoulder for a moment. Z'Nia smiled.

Finally, she began walking again. The crows wheeled slowly above them, still keeping watch.

Z'Nia had traveled miles closer to their destination when she heard a distant *crack.*

"What's that?" James asked.

A gunshot, she said. *The hunters are not nearby. But bullets can travel a long way.*

"I won't let them hurt you," he said again.

Z'Nia smiled. *Thank you, James. I know you would protect me if you could. But no one can stop a bullet once it has been fired.*

"Not even you?"

Not even me. So now we must be extra quiet.

She moved away from the sound of gunshots, but that also took her farther from the hollow. So she circled around to approach from a different direction, all the while listening for human conversations.

Without warning, a flock of birds rose into the air, their black wings flapping noisily.

She wondered, *What frightened them?*

Then she heard a shout. "There!"

Z'Nia whirled. Some distance away, a hunter raised his gun and pointed it at her. An instant later, she heard a loud *bang*. Chips of bark flew from a tree a few feet away.

Intent on reaching the hollow, she'd allowed a human to catch her by surprise. How could she have been so stupid?

Instantly, she felt the anger burning inside her. Ancient instincts urged her to stand and fight.

Fight!

And then she looked down. James stared back at her, trembling.

Worried he might feel the fierce pounding of the blood within her veins, she forced herself to breathe normally. She managed a smile. The anger began to evaporate.

Z'Nia ducked behind a tree. Already, she could hear footsteps pounding toward her.

"What was it?" someone shouted.

"Don't know. Bear, I think. Something big, anyway."

She ran faster than she'd ever run before. They'd hear her, she knew, but that couldn't be helped. All her energy went into escaping this danger. Eventually, she slowed enough to take evasive actions, doubling back on her path and moving onto rocky ground that would conceal her tracks. But she didn't rest until she and James were well away from the hunters.

Z'Nia paused, breathing hard, to look down into his face. His wide eyes and parted lips betrayed his fear.

We are safe now, she told him. *But the day grows short. We must find shelter for the night.*

Tears spilled down his cheeks. "You said I could go home."

I know. Tomorrow will be better.

"I want to go home," he whispered. He turned his face away.

That night, while James slept, Z'Nia worried. She had been careless today and had barely escaped from the hunters. Her lack of attention had endangered not only herself, but James. That must not happen again.

Just as important, however, was her concern about exposing him to her own anger. Three times she had controlled it, but she feared it would become stronger. If it did, she might be unable to master it. She might even harm James. Unwilling to risk his safety, Z'Nia promised herself she would return him to his family without delay, even if it put her in danger. Even danger from guns.

The next morning, Z'Nia took James and headed away from the hollow. She hoped they'd find help by going in a new direction. And only a few hours later, she heard a chorus of friendly voices.

She sent a message into the child's mind. *There are humans nearby. I think they may help you.*

His eyes glowed with hope.

Do you trust me? she asked.

He nodded.

Then please listen carefully. If all goes well, you will leave me now. Say nothing about me. Can you do that?

He nodded again.

"But why?" he whispered.

Because bad men will come for me. They will shoot me or lock me up. Then there will be no one to help the birds and the animals, no one to heal the trees and plants. Promise to say nothing about me.

"I promise."

Satisfied, Z'Nia moved nearer until she could see the humans. A group of boys had camped in a clearing. All much older than James, they wore green shirts with bright-colored patches.

An adult cautioned the boys to avoid harming the plants and trees. Instead of building a fire for cooking, he said they'd use a stove to safeguard the environment.

Z'Nia liked his words. She decided she could trust this human.

He will help you, she said. And she told James what to do.

Minutes later, he walked out of the forest, alone and unharmed. In his hands, he carried a perfect pinecone and an ancient arrowhead. He walked up to the boys.

"My name is James Braden," he said. "I'm lost, and I want to go home."

Z'Nia watched and listened from fifty yards away. She saw James look into the forest and knew his eyes searched for her. She took care that they did not find her.

The boys seemed excited. They pulled down their tents and packed their equipment. Her vision blurred by tears, Z'Nia watched them march away. She sent James one last thought.

Good-bye. Be safe.

Then Z'Nia went back behind the waterfall. She found some pigments and painted a picture of James on the wall of her cave. It showed him smiling and holding her hand.

I'll never forget you, she said.

Somewhere outside, quite far away, a gunshot echoed. Z'Nia stiffened.

Would James keep his promise? She thought he would try. But could such a tiny cub understand what she'd asked him to do? Would he remember? Had he told someone about her already?

Bang! Another gunshot, a little closer.

A crow responded with a mournful cry.

The sound seemed to pierce her soul. Z'Nia felt her fury ignite once more, stronger than ever. She sprang to her feet, prepared for any assault. A low growl exploded from the depths of her throat and echoed through the cave.

Her eyes widened in shock. One hand flew to her mouth, as if she might somehow swallow that awful cry. She felt confused. Ashamed.

This is wrong, she thought. *Why is this happening to me? I cannot- I must not-*

But she couldn't seem to form the words she needed.

I thought you said you could handle this, Mother's voice reminded her.

Z'Nia gasped from the effort of trying to focus. *How can I meditate if I cannot think? Tell me what to do.*

But her mother offered no advice.

Z'Nia sank onto her knees before the fire. She looked up at the pictures on the wall, mentally naming each one.

Sun ... tree ... bird ... deer.

Finally, she saw a picture of herself holding the hand of a small human child. And it was there she found her focus.

She began to chant, *I am a Tazsmin, perhaps the last of my species. I care for the earth and all of its creatures. I am a Tazsmin, perhaps the last of my species-*

Z'Nia banked the fire, her hands trembling. She repeated her chant over and over until the urge for conflict finally passed. Then she sat in the shadows, wearily listening to the hunters closing in and wondering if they would find her today.

Six Years Later

⤬⤬ ⤬⤬ ⤬⤬

CHAPTER 6
Lindsey

Lindsey looked at her fingernails, frowning. Her mother sold beauty products and had given Lindsey a sample bottle of "Sizzling Pink" polish. The color looked okay, but she hadn't done the best job of applying it. As so frequently happened, her mind had been on her younger brother.

What's he up to now? she kept wondering.

Nearly six years after James mysteriously disappeared and then came back, she continued to worry about him.

It wasn't your fault, her parents had said.

But Lindsey knew it was. They had asked her to bring James, and she had failed.

She often relived the events of that day. The problems had started when Mother fell and couldn't walk down to the car.

I'll have to help her, Daddy had said. *Josh can bring the basket and the blanket. And, Lindsey, you bring James.*

She'd meant to be responsible. She had called James and seen him start walking toward her. But then Josh had needed help to fold the blanket, and of course she knew how it should be done. And when they'd finished, James was gone.

I bet he went after Mom and Dad, Josh had said.

Lindsey had believed him.

She'd looked around before leaving the hollow. Something bright red lay there on the grass. James's favorite rubber ball. That, she'd grabbed. But her brother? Oh, no. Him, she'd managed to leave behind.

Only upon reaching the car had she realized the truth. James was missing. And no amount of searching or screaming his name had been able to bring him back. Until three days later, that is. Somehow, he'd just turned up, all by himself.

James wouldn't say where he'd been during those missing days. Not then, and not now. Lindsey felt sure someone had taken him. The Boy Scouts had found James miles away from the Bradens' picnic spot.

A three-year-old couldn't have walked that far, she thought for the hundredth time. *And when the Scouts brought him back, he wasn't hungry or tired or dirty. He didn't even seem upset. Somebody must have helped him. Probably the same person who took him in the first place.*

What if James had gone with that person willingly? Kids had been known to do that. They'd take candy from a stranger or help someone find a lost puppy. Maybe that was what had happened to James. And what if that person came after him again?

Lindsey's greatest fear was that her brother would disappear a second time and never return. Now, whenever she could, she kept an eye on him. She followed him to school each morning and home again in the afternoon. It would be easier if he'd walk with her, but he refused.

I'm almost nine, he'd told her, as if that meant no one could harm him now. Lindsey knew better.

So as James walked to and from school, she trailed half a block behind, ready to yell if a stranger appeared. Though she hadn't seen anything suspicious yet, she'd been puzzled by some of the things James did when he thought no one was watching.

For one thing, he had a way with animals. Every dog on the block wagged its tail when James walked by, and all the cats came to rub against his legs. Shadow, the Bradens' dog, ignored commands from Lindsey or Josh but would do any trick James asked him to do.

Roll over. Sit up. Play dead.

Anything.

James also sang to their mother's flowers, the same meaningless words over and over again. Mom said he had a green thumb. Lindsey thought they just liked his singing.

He often muttered in his sleep, too. Something about guns and cavemen. That made no sense at all because Lindsey knew guns didn't even exist during the time of cave dwellers.

Now he'd joined the Cub Scouts, of all things. That was a real surprise because he'd never liked group activities.

Lindsey did, though. She thought wistfully of the dance class she'd quit because the practice schedule prevented her from watching James walk home from school. She'd dropped flute lessons for the same reason.

It's not fair.

That's how she felt sometimes, though she'd never say it aloud. She wished she could just live her own life and give up watching over James. But she couldn't bring herself to do that.

She knew her parents had noticed. She'd heard them talking.

It's an obsession, her father had said.

Lindsey liked big words. She had looked it up on Word Bounce, her favorite vocabulary website. She learned it meant "preoccupied" and "unreasonable."

Dad's wrong, she thought. *I may be preoccupied with keeping James safe, but there's nothing unreasonable about it.*

Her mother understood. She worried about James, too. Still, Mom often urged Lindsey to be patient.

James keeps things to himself, Mom would say. *If you ask too many questions, he'll just clam up. Give him time.*

Lindsey didn't want to wait.

Why did he choose the Cub Scouts? she asked herself again. *And why now?*

She concluded that James was definitely up to something.

ᘒᘐ   ᘒᘐ   ᘒᘐ

James

"When will we go camping?" James asked his den leader.

"That'll happen after you move on to the Boy Scouts," Mr. Jessup replied. "We'll take some hikes, though."

James had attended several Scout meetings. Mostly, the boys played games or practiced survival skills. James enjoyed those activities, but he'd had another reason for joining the Scouts. He wanted to see Z'Nia again.

He'd never forgotten her. Over the years, he'd paged through dozens of books on animals, hoping to see her picture. He didn't find her. He also searched among the primates at the zoo, but she wasn't there, either.

Then, about a month ago, a Boy Scout recruiting flier had caught his eye.

I remember those guys, he'd thought.

A troop of Boy Scouts had "found" him all those years ago. He remembered seeing a newspaper headline that said, "Local Scouts Find Missing Boy."

Mom kept the news clipping in a book called *Dealing with Childhood Trauma*. Every so often, James opened the book to look at the article. Though reading it didn't help him find Z'Nia, it did keep his memories alive. And it reminded him that the Scouts sometimes went camping. Maybe they'd camp near Z'Nia's home.

He called the number on the flier, but it turned out he didn't meet the age requirement for the Boy Scouts. So he joined the Cub Scouts instead.

When his den practiced tying knots, James remembered a rope he and Z'Nia had woven from vines. When they took turns walking a balance beam, he pretended to inch along a fallen tree to cross a river. And when they learned about birds, he watched for a sparrow with a slightly imperfect left wing. He didn't see one, but he hoped it still lived. And he hoped Z'Nia continued to watch over it.

Late in the summer, the Cub Scouts finally planned a hike. He was excited to hear they'd be going to a state park near his family's old picnic site.

Maybe I can sneak away from the other guys long enough to find Z'Nia, he thought.

But his parents refused to sign the consent form.

"It's not like we're going by ourselves," James said. "Mr. Jessup will be with us the whole time."

His mother was sorting the beauty products her customers had ordered. Dad was using the Internet to research reviews of a new Sci-Fi movie.

Hey! Listen to me! James wanted to say. Knowing his parents probably wouldn't appreciate that, he tried to be patient.

"Eleven, twelve, thirteen– Where's that other lipstick?" his mother mumbled. She wrote something on a note pad. Then she looked up at him and shook her head.

"Not this time, James," she said. Apparently she'd been paying attention after all.

"But Mom, Dad—"

His father looked away from the computer screen. He held up one hand to end the discussion.

"No, James. That's final," he said.

James knew his parents worried that he'd disappear again. He'd heard them talking late at night.

How much does he remember? It feels like he's holding something back, one of them would say. *It's almost as if he has a secret.*

And the other one would answer, *Yes, but he's safe, and that's what matters.*

James wished he could tell his parents about Z'Nia, but he couldn't. Not once in all this time had he mentioned her to anyone. And now, because he'd kept his promise, his parents didn't trust him to go on the hike.

He tried again. "Mr. Jessup said we'll see lots of great rock specimens up there. I'll be the only one who has to miss it."

His parents looked at each other. James had been collecting rocks for years now, and they had encouraged him. He held his breath. Maybe they'd give in after all.

"We'll take you," Mom said finally.

"But Mom—"

"I can show you the rocks," his father said.

James couldn't argue that point. His dad was a high school science teacher and probably knew a lot more about rocks than Mr. Jessup did. James pulled Shadow onto his lap and let the dog lick his face while he thought about what to say.

"I'd like to go with my friends," he said finally.

Dad shook his head. "You go with us or not at all. That's the deal. Take it or leave it."

Reluctantly, James agreed. At least for now, he had no better hope of seeing Z'Nia.

On a bright September Sunday, they took a picnic up into the hills to the place his dad still referred to as "the hollow." Josh had baseball practice, and Lindsey was at a party, so James and his parents went by themselves.

Good thing, James thought. *When Lindsey's around, it's like having two moms. She watches me all the time. And Josh would want to play catch the whole afternoon. I have other things to do.*

Mom had wanted to bring Shadow, but James feared the dog would detect Z'Nia's scent. So when Mom invited Shadow to get into the car, James had whispered, "Stay here, boy. I'll take you for a run later."

Shadow had stubbornly refused to leave the yard. James promised himself to make that run an extra long one, but he still felt guilty.

It's what I had to do, he thought as he nibbled at the fruit and sandwiches his mother had packed. Excited because Z'Nia might be somewhere nearby, he could hardly swallow.

"Have a brownie," Mom said.

James thanked her and choked it down, not even tasting the extra chocolate chips he knew she had added just for him.

As he ate, his gaze constantly roved across the hills. Once he saw something move, but it turned out to be a bird. Then he spotted what seemed to be a tuft of hair rising from behind a rock. He soon realized it was just a branch swaying in the wind.

Z'Nia would never come this close while Mom and Dad are here, he thought.

He stretched his arms above his head and said, "I'm full. I think I'll take a walk."

Dad got to his feet. "Good idea. I'll join you. We can look at those rocks you wanted to see."

James had no choice but to let his father come along. He tramped up the hillside and stopped next to Z'Nia's boulder. Beyond it, the hills dipped and then rose again toward a rock-covered ridge line.

"Do you remember this place?" Dad asked.

James squinted at a birch grove. His mind filled with a hazy picture of Z'Nia hiding there.

"Those trees—" he murmured.

He caught himself just in time. "I like them. I wish Grandpa would grow some birches."

His father sighed.

This will never work, James thought. *He won't let me out of his sight.*

"Let's go," he said. He started back toward his mother.

Dad stopped him. "What about the rocks?"

"Oh. Sure."

His dad began talking about some rock formations he found especially interesting. He even took pictures with his cell phone.

James soon stopped paying attention. He thought he heard another voice, one that seemed to be inside his mind. Was it Z'Nia's, or had he imagined it? He couldn't be sure.

"You're not listening," his father said. "What's the matter? You said you wanted to see these rocks."

"I thought I heard something," James replied. "But I guess not."

Disappointed, James remained alert for that other voice while his father pointed out samples of limestone and shale. He kept listening even after they had gone back to help Mom pack up the leftovers. He didn't hear it again.

Soon it was time to leave. James paused for one last look at the hollow. He saw a lush meadow with gentle hills rising all around. On its eastern side, the grass ended abruptly at an exposed rock face. Beside it, the path wound up the slope to that line of boulders at the top. Nothing more. No Z'Nia. He turned away.

When they got home, James saw Lindsey kneeling in the flower bed, looking for dead blossoms on the geranium plants. He knew she wouldn't find any. Mom picked them off each morning.

She's really waiting for us, he thought. *Probably just wants to check up on me.*

Lindsey told Mom the party had broken up early. She stared at James as if attempting to read his mood. He stomped up the front walk, not even trying to hide his bad temper.

"Did you have a good trip?" Lindsey asked when he walked by.

He ignored her. He didn't want to talk.

"I asked you—"

James turned to face her.

"Fine," he said. "Just great. Now leave me alone."

As he went into the house, he heard Lindsey ask their mother whether anything unusual had happened.

"No," Mom said. "Nothing."

James slammed the door.

She's right, he thought. *Nothing happened. Not one thing. I guess I'll never see Z'Nia again.*

CHAPTER 7

Z'Nia

Z'Nia's mother had taught her to value work above everything else. And work filled Z'Nia's days just as it always had. But it didn't fill her heart, not any more. Though she still loved the life of the Tazsmin, her work was no longer enough. She missed James. She missed answering his questions and teaching him the ways of living things. She missed having someone to talk to.

She wondered what Mother would say about that.

Most likely, Mother would say, *Do the work, Daughter. Your work is far more important than any human.*

Z'Nia sighed and did her work.

She lived in the cave behind the waterfall most of the time now. She liked waking up in the morning and seeing James's picture there on the wall. It smiled down at her while she ate her morning meal. It focused her thoughts as she completed her daily meditation. And every time she went out to do her work, she carried that image in her mind.

Whenever she placed her hands on an injured animal or a damaged plant, she imagined smaller hands resting next to hers. When she sang her wind-soft words of healing, she pretended to hear James's voice singing along.

This is nonsense, Mother's voice would scold her.

And Z'Nia would reply, *You taught me to find joy in my work. For that, I will always be grateful, Mother. But James gave me something more. He helped me find joy in living.*

That was why, several times each month, Z'Nia journeyed to the little hollow in the hills. It had become one of her favorite spots. She never really expected to see James there, but she always hoped that she might.

Today, she'd risen early. Something had told her she must visit the hollow before midday. She'd felt a sort of mental pull. Her connection to James had tightened like someone tugging gently on a rope. When the sun touched her waterfall and left a rainbow in each crystal drop, she had set off.

She had walked through the forest, noting the scent of wild strawberries, hearing the wind whisper its secrets while the birds called out greetings. *Caw. Caw.*

Z'Nia had heard the human voices long before she got to the hollow.

It might be hunters, she'd reminded herself as her pulse quickened. *It could be hikers or campers or forest rangers. It might be anyone.*

This time, she had decided, she would be cautious. She had stayed well back among the trees and parted the branches just enough to allow her a view that made her gasp. After all these years, James had returned. She'd been disappointed so many times that the sight of him left her astonished.

When a black bird drifted over to settle comfortably upon her shoulder, she'd felt glad of its company. She had news to share.

He is here, she had whispered.

And then, though the bird had made no reply, she'd added, *He has grown.*

In fact, James had changed a great deal. His hair had darkened to a chestnut shade, and his rounded baby features had morphed into a firm chin and high cheekbones. The top of his head nearly reached his father's shoulder. She'd seen the two of them coming in her direction and knew she'd have to move if they got too close.

But James and his father had climbed only to the boulders at the top of the lower hill. Even from a distance, she'd been able to hear parts of their conversation.

"Do you remember this place?" the father had asked.

"Those trees … I wish Grandpa would grow some birches."

He still talks about his grandpa's trees, she'd thought, feeling pleased.

Knowing it would not be safe to move closer, Z'Nia had resisted the temptation. James had started back toward his mother anyway.

So she'd sent him a mental message, just a simple, *Hello. I missed you.*

He'd paused there on the hillside, and at first, she'd thought he might have heard. But he never raised his head or looked around. Sadly, she'd wondered if James could no longer receive and understand her mind-link.

All the same, she had been delighted to see him. She'd studied him carefully, noting his straight posture and the firmness of his steps. She'd watched as he helped gather the family's belongings and obediently followed his parents. Before he left the hollow, he had turned once more for a single long look.

Good-bye, she had said as she watched him leave, though she doubted he heard it.

The bird flew off after him. When it returned a few minutes later, she knew James was truly gone.

Now she felt a stab of sadness.

Mother, on the other hand, seemed glad that he had left.

Haven't you seen enough? she asked. *How foolish you are, chasing out here to watch that human.*

Not just 'that human.' James.

Still a human. Still our enemy, Mother said. *Go home, daughter.*

Soon. When I am ready.

Despite her mother's objections, Z'Nia stayed there for a long time, watching the spot where James had stood. Seeing him had eased her loneliness, but the feeling seemed bittersweet. She would still miss his company.

Caw. The crow's drawn-out cry recalled her to the present.

I must return to my waterfall, she told herself.

She decided to make a new cave painting of this older James. She would need more pigment, especially yellow, but she knew just where to find it. And she had some twigs she could burn and grind to make the black charcoal she'd need. She visualized the picture she would begin that evening.

In the midst of her thoughts, she heard a sharp *crack* behind her. The sound of a twig breaking. Her eyes widened.

Z'Nia spun around, ready to run for her life. Only a few paces from her stood four adult human males. Each man carried a gun.

"Now!" one of them shouted, gesturing for the others to move so they could surround her.

"Don't kill it!" somebody yelled.

One man raised his gun to his shoulder and swung it like a club. Z'Nia batted it away. But the others closed in, and all four men began showering her with blows. She dodged. She twisted. She tried to escape. Nothing worked.

I cannot fight so many, she thought.

Z'Nia's heartbeat slammed inside her chest. Her throat ached from gasping.

Mother, help me!

But her mother offered no suggestions. Z'Nia felt as if she had been abandoned.

From a nearby tree, the crow shrieked a war cry. It seemed to carry all the old warnings: *Be cautious. Never trust. They will kill you.*

Z'Nia wanted to bite and kick and tear at her attackers. She tried to summon up the hot anger that would help her fight. But the years of meditation had buried those instincts so deeply she could not find them.

Despairing, Z'Nia screamed.

The men fell back at the sound but only for a moment. Before she could take even one step, the largest of the men swung his gun directly at her head. She tried to duck, but her body felt heavy and slow.

The weapon connected with a *smack*.

Z'Nia felt a splitting pain in her temple. It throbbed and grew until she feared her head might burst. She staggered sideways and made a feeble grab at a tree, but her hand slipped away. She fell to the ground, dazed.

The bird flew above her, calling out some message she could not understand. Tiny lights danced before her eyes. She raised one hand as if to catch them.

Has the sun gone down? she wondered. *I can see the stars.*

Then the night sky must have swallowed them up. Or perhaps the crow had done so. The stars disappeared, and Z'Nia saw nothing more except the blackness.

The Present

CHAPTER 8

James

"James, you'll be late," his mother called.

James clattered downstairs, one hand swinging a battered duffel bag. He paused at the hallway mirror to finger-comb hair that had darkened to a deep brown. His brother's face appeared in the mirror behind him. The boys looked alike, though Josh was more solidly built. Josh clutched a football with his left hand and used the other to jam his baseball cap onto James's head.

"Hey!" James began.

"Just trying to save you some work," Josh said. "Your hair's hopeless anyway, little brother."

"Who are you calling little?" James asked. He threw the cap at Josh.

They both grinned. They'd repeated variations of this ritual many times over the past several months. Right after his twelfth birthday, James had shot up four inches. Their dad liked to joke that the two boys could almost "see eye to eye" on everything now.

Mom called again, "James, your father needs to leave soon."

The boys stopped their good-natured jostling and went into the kitchen. The smell of bacon and eggs greeted them. Their mother loved to cook and made them a big breakfast nearly every day.

"Dad's going to drop you off at school on his way to work," she told James as she scooped scrambled eggs onto his plate. "He'll help you carry your science fair project inside."

"Okay."

James went to the kitchen counter. He nudged aside a trio of pale blue shopping bags, each with the words "Wake Up to Beauty" angling across it in gold script. Behind Mom's cosmetic orders stood his tray of bean plants.

James had grown the plants from seeds. He'd played classical music for half of them, keeping the other conditions the same for all the seedlings. The "music lovers," as he called them, had grown inches taller than those raised without music. He had one more plant in his room, an even larger one that he hadn't included in his project. Rather than playing the classical music, James had sung to it every day. He'd learned the song from Z'Nia.

Even after nine years, he hadn't forgotten her, but he could no longer picture her face. He could no longer hear the words of her mind-link, either. Only the song remained to him, that and a sense that he'd lost something precious.

His mother's voice broke into his thoughts. "Come have something to eat."

James sat down next to Lindsey. As always, his sister's hair and nails looked perfect. Even her carefully frayed jeans were wrinkle-free. She had already finished her breakfast and was stacking her books according to size.

Lindsey's attention to detail sometimes drove James crazy. He rolled his eyes. Josh grinned.

James poured some orange juice. He took a bite of eggs but avoided the bacon his mother had cooked. As he'd gotten older, he'd felt less and less interested in eating meat. Many days he ate none at all.

Z'Nia didn't eat meat, he thought, glad to remember even that small detail.

"Hey," Josh said. He pointed at the bacon. "You want that?"

James shook his head, knowing his athlete brother could easily devour a second helping.

"You should eat that bacon, James," Lindsey said. "Regina Simon told me protein helps you think. It might improve your chances at the science fair today."

"No, thanks." James drank some juice and bit into his toast.

Lindsey persisted. "You could just try it. After all, Regina's mom is a nurse. She says the right breakfast gives your day a good start."

James had learned to tune out the frequent health advice Lindsey gave him, all passed on from her best friend Regina. Ignoring her comment, he slid the bacon onto Josh's plate.

Lindsey sighed and flicked an imaginary speck of lint from her sleeve.

Dad hurried into the kitchen, his dark hair still wet from the shower. He tucked his laptop beneath one arm, grabbed his briefcase, and picked up James's science fair poster with his free hand.

"Let's go," he said. His first class at the high school started in just forty-five minutes.

James gulped down some more eggs, then pushed away from the table. Shadow instantly appeared. The black border collie looked up at him expectantly.

"Sit up," James said. "Come on, Shadow, beg."

The dog immediately sat back on his haunches and put up his paws to beg for food. James rewarded him with a big bite of toast.

"Good boy," he said, and he patted the dog's head.

Then, balancing the plant tray against his body, he started for the car.

"Have you got everything?" his mother called after him.

"Yes, Mom."

"Because you're staying over at Matt's tonight."

"Yeah, I packed some stuff. See?"

He hoisted the duffel bag.

"What about—"

"I've got it, Mom. I have everything I need."

He came back to kiss her cheek. It smelled of rose-scented soap.

"I'm not in kindergarten anymore," he teased.

She smiled at him. "I'm sorry. Have a good time at Matt's."

"I will," he said. Then he left.

Hours later, James walked home from school with Matt Oliver. They'd met in Cub Scouts three years before and had been best friends ever since.

Matt's sandy hair, green eyes, and freckled nose gave him a mischievous look that matched his personality. Thanks to that recent growth spurt, James was several inches taller than his friend. Matt didn't seem to care. He said he'd catch up next year.

James stopped in front of the post office to pick up a shiny pebble he'd spotted on the sidewalk.

"Quartz," he muttered. He put it in his pocket, intending to add it to his rock collection.

"Too bad you didn't have that stone this morning," Matt said. "You could have thrown it at Jeff Pearson's iguana."

James snorted. "Don't think it would have helped much. Lucky that thing was just a baby, or Brittany Barnes would have fainted."

He smiled at the memory of today's science class. Brittany had stood on her chair while James, Matt, and some of the other boys helped Jeff chase down the escaped lizard.

"It did make the science fair interesting," James said. "Jeff should have gotten extra points for the most exciting project."

"Yeah, but yours was still the best," Matt replied. Though his own model volcano had failed to erupt on cue, he'd cheerfully congratulated James on a first-place ribbon.

"Thanks," James said.

They were approaching the Celebrations Gift Shop. With Halloween less than a week away, the owner had filled the front window with orange and black decorations. However, a bright yellow poster now hung there, too. James wandered over to look at it.

"Hey, what's this?"

Matt trailed after him so he could read the flier. "A circus?"

"Yep. Right here in Tyler's Ferry," James said.

His gaze met Matt's in the shiny glass reflection. The boys grinned at each other.

"Let's go!" they both said.

They dropped their school books at Matt's house. After checking in with his mom, they grabbed a couple of bikes from the big front porch and took off. They raced across residential streets and skimmed through the downtown. Finally, they made the turnoff onto Old Highway 187.

Minutes later, they skidded to a stop with a spray of gravel. Other kids had arrived earlier, mostly seventh- and eighth-grade boys. They all stared across the road at the vacant lot.

"For Sale or Lease—12 Acres," read the sign posted there. Surrounded on three sides by overgrown woodland, the lot extended along several hundred yards of roadway. It held only a concrete slab, foundation for a restaurant that had never been built. Now that the new highway across town left Old 187 largely unused, no one seemed to want this lot. Until today.

"What are they doing?" James asked.

An older boy scowled at him. "They gotta put everything up, don't they? What a dumb question."

James shrugged and ignored the comment. Other than friendly wrestling matches with Josh, he'd never been in a fight, and he planned to keep it that way. Besides, he couldn't see the point in getting angry over stuff like this. His dad said some things were worth fighting for, but James didn't know what they might be. He and Matt both found it easier to just stay away from people who wanted to cause trouble.

They watched as dozens of men pulled on ropes that would anchor a massive tent to the ground. Other men were unloading equipment from large trucks. James saw everything from wooden planks and brightly colored canvas to saddles studded with fake gems. He spotted a herd of animals standing near one of the trucks. Only because the zebras, tigers, and gorillas remained motionless did he he realize they were stuffed. From a distance, they looked life-like.

"I didn't expect anything this big," he said. "I've never seen a circus before."

"Me, neither," Matt said.

A voice came from behind them. "Well, you don't know what you've been missing."

Barry McAfee, one of their classmates, had joined them. James suppressed a sigh.

"Hi, Barry," he said. "I guess you've been—"

"To a circus? I sure have. Ringling Brothers. About the biggest one there is." Barry pushed a tangle of light brown hair away from his eyes. "Personally, I don't think this one looks like much."

Ignoring Barry, Matt continued talking to James. "It's gonna be here tomorrow and Saturday. Think your mom will let you go?"

James thought about his mother's tendency to watch over him. He'd missed plenty of outings because she kept him close to home.

"Well—"

"She probably won't," Barry said. "Remember the time I invited you guys to my birthday camp-out? James couldn't go because he had a cold. At least that's what he said. Personally, I thought that was a lame excuse. Didn't you, Matt?"

Matt didn't answer.

I really did have a cold, James thought. *A little one anyway. And this is different. I'm older now.*

"I can go," he said. "No problem."

Across the road, two men erected a wooden sign proclaiming "Slade's Amazing Circus Escapades!"

"What's an escapade anyway?" Matt asked.

"A trick maybe? You know, like circus tricks," James said.

"Oh. Well, I never heard of it."

"It's sure not Ringling Brothers," Barry said. "Pretty small. Personally, I'm not impressed."

James frowned. "Maybe it's small, but it's still a circus. And I'm going."

"Me, too," Matt said. "Personally."

Barry didn't seem to notice the sarcasm. James and Matt grinned at each other over his head.

After a while, most of the kids got bored and left. James and Matt remained, leaning on their handlebars to stare at the tent and the bright flags streaming from its peak. And no matter how they ignored him, Barry stayed right there with them.

Suddenly, James heard a voice. "Hey! You boys!"

He looked around. Only he, Matt, and Barry were still there.

"Guess he means us," James said. "Did we do something wrong?"

"Gotta go," Barry said, and he took off in a hurry.

Matt cheered softly. "About time! I thought he'd never leave."

"Yeah," James replied with a grin. "Maybe we should text him a thank-you message."

Matt laughed and punched James on the shoulder.

Then both boys turned their attention to the man approaching them from across the highway. They recognized Mr. Hardin, a big man who wore wire-rimmed glasses and a solid-gold pinky ring. He lived two doors down from the Olivers.

"What's he doing here?" James muttered.

"Mr. Hardin owns this lot," Matt told him. "He must have rented it to the circus."

"We didn't do anything," he called to his neighbor.

Mr. Hardin laughed. "No, no, I just wondered if you and your friend would like to earn some money. Here's ten dollars each if you'll hang these fliers around town."

"Deal," Matt said.

He grabbed the fliers and a roll of tape, pocketed his ten dollar bill, and passed the other to James.

James took one of the fliers. He saw a blurry photo and dark text.

"Read it later," Matt said. "There must be a hundred posters here, and Mom's expecting us back before dinner."

They got busy taping fliers to light poles, mailboxes, and the sides of buildings. By sunset, they had nearly finished.

Matt suggested they split up. "You hang these two fliers over on Oak Street. I'll put the others near that new bank. We'll meet back at my house."

Eager to finish ahead of Matt, James grabbed four strips of tape and took off for Oak Street. He attached one poster to the side of a dumpster. The last one would go on the community bulletin board at the end of the block. About to tape it up, he remembered he hadn't had a chance to read it yet.

He squinted to make out the headline and read it aloud. "See the Only Living Bigfoot in Captivity!"

Below the spiky lettering, a dark and grainy picture showed a creature raising long-fingered hands to hide from the camera.

Bigfoot's a myth, he said to himself. *Otherwise, scientists would be all over this thing.*

He stared at the paper. The longer he looked at it, the more he began to wonder. Could it be Z'Nia?

No, it can't be. She'd never have let humans get close enough to capture her.

His memory brought up a dim picture of Z'Nia, and with it came doubt. Instead of hanging the flier, he stuffed it into his pocket.

I'll find out, he thought. *Tonight, I'll go see if it's her. Just in case.*

CHAPTER 9

James

James held his wristwatch in front of his face. The watch was waterproof and shock-proof and had numerous other features. Most important, it had a luminous dial.

Just past midnight, he thought. *Perfect.*

He rolled out of bed, pulled his jeans on over his pajamas, and tiptoed across Matt's room. After easing the door open, he slipped into the upstairs hallway. He went downstairs, put on his jacket and shoes, then went out to the front porch.

James pushed one of the bikes down the steps to the lawn and started to mount it. Then Matt's voice came out of the darkness.

"Where do you think you're going?"

Matt must have followed him. James couldn't tell him the truth. Behind his back, he crossed his fingers.

"Home," he said. "I'm not feeling so good."

"Sure. Guess that's why you had two desserts. Mom'll be upset that her cooking made you sick."

"No, dinner was great. I just—" He couldn't explain this, not even to Matt. "I can't tell you."

"Okay, then don't. It doesn't matter. I'm coming with you anyway."

"No, you're not."

"Yeah, I am. Unless you want me to tell Mom and Dad you're leaving. Of course, Mom'll call your parents, and they'll come over here to pick you up. You'll probably get grounded, too. Your mom's pretty strict."

"So is yours," James said. "If we get caught, you'll be in just as much trouble as I will."

"So let's not get caught."

Matt moved closer, pushing a bicycle. He nudged the kickstand up with his toe.

"Which way are we headed?" he asked.

With an exasperated sigh, James wheeled his bike into the street and swung his leg over the crossbar. Matt followed. They pedaled slowly, using the shadows for cover. Police cars sometimes cruised this neighborhood.

If they spot us, they'll call our parents, James thought. No way he'd let that happen.

He gave thanks that a wall of clouds hid the full moon, but he wished he could use his headlamp. Darkness made riding his bike much more difficult. Homeowners had piled mounds of autumn leaves at the curb for pickup. Once, his bike skidded on a drift of leaves, and only Matt's steadying hand saved him from falling.

"Thanks," James muttered.

He pedaled onward, retracing the route they'd taken that afternoon.

After a while, Matt said, "Let me guess. We're going back to the circus."

James didn't answer.

"Okay, you don't have to tell me. I'll see soon enough."

James knew that before long Matt would know exactly where they were going. But the important thing was to keep him from figuring out why. Wasn't it?

He debated with himself. *I promised Z'Nia I wouldn't tell anyone about her. And I've kept my promise for nine years. But Matt's my best friend. He'd never harm her, and I might need help. Should I tell him?*

He worried about it as they rode through quiet streets where dry leaves skipped across their path. He worried some more as they went through the downtown, ignoring traffic lights that blinked like yellow eyes at each deserted intersection. Even when they braked to a stop on Old Highway 187, he still hadn't decided what to do.

Across the road, the big top loomed against the night sky. James saw few security lights and no guards at all, but he knew that could change. This might be his best chance to see Z'Nia.

If it is Z'Nia, he reminded himself.

Finally, Matt spoke, "You gonna tell me why we're here?"

James made a quick decision. "All right, but you gotta promise not to tell."

"Okay."

"No, you gotta swear, Matt. It's really important."

"I swear. I won't tell anyone."

James reached into his pocket, brought out the crumpled flier, and handed it to Matt along with a mini-flashlight.

Matt trained the miniature beam on the paper. His forehead wrinkled in disbelief.

"You came all this way in the middle of the night to see bigfoot? Couldn't we have waited until tomorrow?"

"Bigfoot's a myth," James said.

"I know. So why'd we come out here?"

James took a deep breath. "You heard about how I disappeared when I was three?"

Matt nodded.

And then James told him the story. Almost all of it.

Matt heard him out, but James could see the doubt in his eyes.

"Come on," Matt said. "You expect me to believe you spent three days with bigfoot?"

"Her name's not bigfoot. It's Z'Nia."

"How do you know? Could she talk?"

"No," James said hastily. "She made sounds. Just enough to tell me what to call her. And it's not bigfoot."

"Yeah, okay, whatever. But you really spent three days with her and came out without a scratch?"

James shook his head. "You don't understand."

Guess I made the wrong decision after all, he thought.

He wished he hadn't told Matt the truth. He wished he could take it all back and pretend he'd been joking, but Matt would never buy that.

"Go home," James said. "I'll be there later, but don't say anything to your parents, okay?"

He turned his back.

"Wait," Matt said. "Don't get mad. It's just hard to believe. 'Cause, like you said, bigfoot's a myth."

"And like I also said, she's not bigfoot. And she's not violent, either. She's peaceful. You know, a pacifist."

"Okay, okay, I believe you." Matt looked thoughtful. "But you don't remember where she lived, right?"

"No, just out in the woods somewhere."

"Well, then," Matt said, "I guess you can't go see if she's still there. So you'll have to check out this 'bigfoot' the circus is advertising."

James felt relieved. "Right."

"How will you know if it's really her?" Matt asked.

"I just will."

"But how?"

James hadn't told Matt about the mind-link, but he felt sure Z'Nia would contact him. If it was her, that is.

"You'll have to trust me on that," he said.

Matt sighed. "Fine, don't tell me. So, how do we do this? I mean, do you have a plan?"

"Not really." James pulled at a frayed edge on his jacket cuff while he thought it over. "I guess I'll just sneak over there and look around until I find her."

"And then what?"

James knew if he found Z'Nia, he'd want to release her. He also knew that might not be easy.

"Maybe we should find her first and then decide what to do," he said. "If it's not her, we won't have to worry about it."

"Okay," Matt said. "Whatever you want."

They left their bikes in the shadows beneath a billboard and ran across the highway, their sneakers slapping softly against the asphalt. James didn't stop until he reached a pool of darkness near the big top.

He pointed left. "Let's go that way."

Matt circled his thumb and index finger into an "okay" sign and followed James. They stayed close to the big top, carefully stepping around rope coils and bales of yellow straw. Just before they reached the corner of the tent, they heard voices. Without a sound, they dropped onto the dewy grass and scooted deeper into the shadows.

"Everything all set?" a raspy voice asked.

James heard the sound of a match striking, and a moment later, he smelled cigarette smoke.

"Thanks for the light, Mr. Slade," a deeper voice replied. "Yeah, we're in pretty good shape. You can see we set up the big top and bleachers, and the concessions are ready to go. The animals are all fed and watered, too. All except bigfoot. She ain't eatin' much."

"I know. And people won't pay to see a bigfoot that's half-starved."

What does he mean by that? James thought. *They should be taking better care of her.*

He started to stand up, intending to confront them, but Matt held him back. The men went on talking.

"She ain't half starved. More like underfed," the other man protested.

"Whatever."

"So what're you gonna do, Boss?"

Slade coughed several times.

"Gotta quit these things," he said. He coughed again before he continued. "We've tried to make her eat. It's a waste of time. I'll have to find a new attraction. Maybe a tightrope walker or a sword swallower. I'll start calling around tomorrow. You remember that guy, Branzini?"

"You mean The Great Blandino?"

"That's it, Blandino. He looked pretty good. I'll give him a call."

"But what about bigfoot?"

A cigarette arced to the ground as one of the men tossed it away. Inches from James's face, a scuffed brown boot stamped out the embers.

Slade coughed again. "What about her?"

"Well, if you get Blandino, then you won't need her anymore. Ain't that right?"

"That's right," Slade replied. "You want me to spell it out for you? We're gonna get rid of her right after we play this town. Somewhere between here and Richland, we'll leave her by the side of the road."

"But there's bears around that area. She ain't strong enough to fight 'em off."

Slade laughed. "I might enjoy seeing that."

What's the matter with him? James thought angrily.

He started to get to his feet but felt a hand tighten on his arm. In the darkness, he could barely see his friend. Matt shook his head, telling him this was not the time to reveal their presence.

He's probably right, James thought. Reluctantly, he settled back to listen as Slade started talking again.

"Don't go soft on me, Buddy," he said. "She's just an animal. Bears gotta eat, too, don't they? Besides, she's my property. I have a right to do whatever I want with my own property."

James clenched his teeth until his jaw hurt. He couldn't believe what he'd just heard. Z'Nia was not property.

Buddy continued arguing with his boss. "But Mr. Slade—"

"But nothing. I don't want to hear it. You just make sure no one sees her. I don't want our customers calling up that animal cruelty place and complaining. We treated bigfoot plenty good. It's not our fault she won't eat, is it?"

There was a pause. "I guess not."

"Right. So get her cage loaded on one of the trucks."

"Keep her in there for two whole days? There's not enough air. If someone finds out, there could be trouble. You know, like you said, from those animal cruelty people."

"Okay, okay. Just throw a tarp over her cage. Do it now so you won't forget. And fasten it down tight, you hear?"

"Yes, sir."

One set of footsteps walked away.

"It ain't fair," Buddy said. He let out a sigh.

Then he walked away, too.

James stared after him, torn between his desire to see Z'Nia again and his hope that she wasn't here at all.

"Come on," he whispered. "We have to see where he's going."

Without waiting for Matt's response, he turned the corner. He watched as the man shuffled away. Soon, Buddy's shadow became one among many. Cautiously, James followed him.

CHAPTER 10

James

When he reached the front corner of the tent, James stopped to get his bearings. To his right, a collapsible wooden sign leaned against a ticket booth. The sign listed two evening shows on Friday and two more on Saturday night. The last one would close with a fireworks display.

James saw that the big top formed one side of a rectangle, while various attractions lined the other three sides. Pale moonlight showed him the banners posted above the booths: *Madame Zora, Seer of the Future; Armando's Amazing Sleight-of-Hand Tricks; The Incredible Igor Walks on Glass.*

Above his head, plastic flags snapped in the breeze. The wind brought him a whiff of sawdust mingled with an animal scent that reminded him of the zoo. Somewhere in the darkness, a chain clanked as a large body moved restlessly.

James wondered, *Could that be Z'Nia?*

Matt came up behind him and asked, "Where'd he go?"

James pointed. The man called 'Buddy' was walking toward what appeared to be a cluster of animal cages. Barking dogs greeted his approach, but he just waved at them and went on. He fumbled with one of the cages and then tugged a heavy tarpaulin over it. Ten minutes later, he left amid another chorus of barks.

Buddy's footsteps died away.

"Let's go," James said.

He ran from shadow to shadow, with Matt following close behind. Despite their attempts to stay out of sight, the yapping dogs seemed to be tracking their every move.

"Shh," James murmured as he passed them. "Be quiet."

The dogs stopped barking and lay down.

"How'd you do that?" Matt whispered.

But James did not reply. He found a sign lying in the grass. "Bigfoot," it said. No doubt the circus used it to attract customers. Perhaps Buddy had taken it down. However, he hadn't removed the seven-foot tall stuffed gorilla standing next to it.

Z'Nia's not a gorilla, James thought. Uncertainty filled his mind.

He examined the cage. It had solid metal end-panels, one with a padlocked door. A tarp hid its long side walls and stretched across the top of the cage. Buddy had fastened it securely at all four lower corners. If James wanted to see inside the cage, he'd have to slice through one of the ropes.

He pulled out the Swiss Army knife he'd received for his birthday, but before he could begin sawing at the rope, the dogs started barking again. A flashlight beam swung into view, and James and Matt melted into the shadows. A moment later, Buddy climbed the metal steps, opened the padlocked door, and entered the cage.

"Here you go, bigfoot," Buddy crooned. "Here's some nice fresh meat. I planned to cook this for my dinner tonight, but I'm givin' it to you instead. You gotta eat it, okay?"

James inched over until he could see through the open door. Something lay on the floor at the far end of the cage, its face hidden from the bright beam of Buddy's flashlight. He saw reddish-brown hair, snarled and darkened by dirt. A hand with long fingers pushed away the steak that had been offered.

Matt poked him and raised his eyebrows to ask a silent question. *Is it her?*

James couldn't be sure.

Z'Nia, is that you? he wondered silently.

To his surprise, he immediately heard the answer in his head.

James? Where are you?

The creature tried to sit up, but that seemed to make Buddy nervous.

"No, you don't," he said. "You stay right there until I'm out of here."

He shoved the meat toward her, backed out of the cage, and locked the door.

Buddy picked up the wooden sign and paused to scold the dogs. They subsided for a moment, then bayed loudly again when he left. His footsteps scuffed away across the grass until he disappeared behind the big top.

"It's her," James said.

The fact that he could now send her messages as well as receive them left him breathless. Maybe it had something to do with being older. He wondered silently about her condition, but she didn't reply.

Okay, what did I do wrong? he asked himself.

Surely he hadn't lost the ability to communicate with her already. What had he done differently this time? After thinking about it, he realized his second attempt had not been focused.

I have to direct the message to her, he guessed. *That means we can't just read each other's thoughts.*

He tried again. *Are you all right?*

I am weak. They bring me mostly meat, and I cannot eat it. I pull leaves from the trees when I can. Sometimes I try to eat the straw they throw inside the cage for my bedding, but it makes me sick.

I'll bring food tomorrow. Can you wait that long?

Yes, of course. James, how did you find me?

He swallowed. He knew his mind-link would seem angry. *I saw one of their fliers. They call you 'bigfoot.'*

Her tone sounded amused. *They do not know I am the last of the Tazsmin.*

Tazsmin? What's that?

You would say 'WindSinger.' It is the name of my species, and it also describes the work we do. I will tell you more about that, but this is not the time.

James became aware of Matt pulling at his arm.

"Hey! Are you in a trance or something? Do you want to cut the rope or not?" Matt asked.

"No. Not tonight."

"Is she okay?"

"She's a vegetarian, and they're giving her meat. She needs better food."

"What should we do?"

James folded the blade on his knife and shoved it into his pocket. "Let me think a minute."

He felt Z'Nia's mind reaching out to his. She wanted to know who had come with him.

A friend. Matt's helping me. We'll get you out of there.

Not now, she told him. *The one called 'Slade' may return soon. He is not a good person.*

What about Buddy? Could he help us?

He is not brave, but he is kind. He brings food twice a day and visits me when the animals are working.

And there's no one else? James asked.

Z'Nia said, *No one who visits often.*

Matt tugged at James again. "What's the matter with you? I said we have to go!"

"What?"

"A police car just pulled up. I think he's doing a security check. We have to get out of here."

"Okay."

James lifted one edge of the tarp and spoke just loudly enough so Matt could hear. "I'll come back tomorrow with some food. And I'll try to have a plan to get you out of there."

He said good-bye and released the tarp, pausing only to quiet the dogs before following Matt.

"You think she understood what you said?" Matt asked.

"She's smart," James replied. "And she's been living with humans for a while now. Yeah, I think she got it."

The boys silently threaded their way back behind the big top and then across the road to find their bikes. An hour later, they crept into the house and went to bed.

Tired but unable to sleep, James lay awake listening to the muted snoring coming from Matt's side of the room. His mind replayed the conversation he'd overheard between Slade and Buddy. He knew Slade didn't care what happened to Z'Nia. To him, she represented an attraction that could bring in money. Nothing more. He had even referred to her as his "property."

James's anger boiled up at the memory. Z'Nia was not a piece of property someone could own! He hated the very idea of her being in a cage. Was this what his dad meant about some things being worth the fight?

Probably, he thought. *But I don't know much about fighting. Maybe Josh could teach me.*

His brother had offered to show him some wrestling moves on multiple occasions. James visualized himself putting a headlock on Slade and realized the notion was ridiculous. There was no way he could take on a grown man. Maybe two grown men, if Buddy decided to help his boss.

There must be something I can do, he thought.

But what? Ideas floated through his mind, and he discarded each one. Too dangerous. Too difficult. Or just plain stupid.

I'll think of something, he promised himself. *I don't care if it takes me all night.*

But despite his intentions, he finally fell asleep.

Matt's alarm buzzed at seven. James woke up in a tangle of blankets, hands gripping his pillow tightly.

He'd had a weird dream about the circus. In his dream, stuffed zebras, tigers, and gorillas were racing wildly through the big top. He and Matt ran out to catch them. But before they could do so, a magician entered the center ring. With a wave of his wand, he made the audience disappear. Only James and Matt remained to lead the animals away.

"Weird," James muttered.

He struggled to recall the rest of the dream. Hadn't there been something about Buddy? But the dream had vanished along with the magician's audience.

He let his thoughts drift again to the problem of how to free Z'Nia. And that was when it hit him, the one way he might be able to do it. But he'd need Matt's help.

Will it work? he wondered.

It might, if he and Matt could figure out all the details. One thing he knew for sure. In less than forty-eight hours, the circus would leave town. If he didn't get her out of that cage, Z'Nia would go with it.

CHAPTER 11

James

James and Matt reached the circus grounds just after five o'clock. Parked cars already filled one end of the vacant lot, and crowds had gathered near the big top.

James carried a white plastic bag from the Thrifty Check Supermarket. It contained packages of salad greens and sprouts, "green stuff" they'd hoped Z'Nia would like. He shoved the bag inside his jacket.

"We've got half an hour," he said. "After that, everybody but us will be watching the show."

That was when James and Matt would bring the food to Z'Nia.

The boys walked around, pretending to be interested in the concessions.

Matt's not pretending, James soon decided.

Matt bought a ticket to see a two-headed goat. He experimented with a mirror that made him look huge if he angled it just right. He tossed Ping-Pong balls at small, round fishbowls and almost won a goldfish. And he even dragged James into a tent to see trained rats run through a maze in search of food.

"Watching those rats made me hungry," Matt said.

He bought a cone of cotton candy, pulled off a strand, and crammed it into his mouth.

"What are you doing?" James finally asked. "We're here to help Z'Nia, not to have fun."

Matt grinned. "I'm trying to be authentic, like I'm really here for the circus. Besides, I'm starving."

James couldn't enjoy food while Z'Nia went hungry, but he bought a soft drink anyway so that he, too, would look "authentic."

The boys continued their aimless walk until they drew near the animal cages. By daylight, they could see three chattering monkeys living in one cage. A drowsy lion with a scrawny mane sprawled on the floor of a second one. Other cages held a baby elephant that would soon outgrow its quarters, a fearful black bear cub, and a half dozen mixed-breed terriers that barked at everyone who passed.

The cages were shabby but very clean, and the animals had plenty of water.

Buddy takes good care of them, James thought.

He heard someone in the crowd complaining, "Where's bigfoot? That's what we came to see."

"Sorry, she's not feeling well," a concession worker replied. "We hope to have her on display again tomorrow."

"Not if I can help it," James muttered.

His anger grew as he eyed the tarp-covered cage. Z'Nia should have been out in the woods doing her work, not locked up like some wild animal. She had done nothing to deserve this.

Matt nudged him. "Calm down. You look like you're ready to pick a fight with somebody, and that's definitely not your thing."

Remembering his thoughts from the previous evening, James almost laughed at that. He unclenched his teeth and tried to relax. Matt was right. Getting angry wouldn't solve anything, and it might even raise suspicions. He forced himself to smile.

"Come on," he said.

Z'Nia's cage now rested directly behind the lion's, so the boys went to look at the sleeping cat. They had planned to slip between the cages now that the crowds had thinned out, but they saw Barry McAfee approaching.

"What's with Barry?" Matt asked. "Is he following us or something?"

"Don't know," James replied. "But we have to watch what we say when he's around."

Barry stopped in front of the lion's cage and regarded the animal critically. "Not too scary, is he?"

"Yeah," James replied. "He does look kind of—"

"Pathetic? He sure does," Barry said.

"I was going to say 'tired.' I bet it's hard to sleep with all these people around."

Barry wasn't finished. "What do you think, Matt? This lion is about as pathetic as your science project, isn't he? Ha-ha! Think he'll 'erupt' any time soon?"

"Well," Matt said, "if you mean, is he going to be sick like that time you threw up in gym class? Yeah, you never know. He might."

"Very funny," Barry said. He backed away from the cage as if he feared Matt's prediction might be correct.

"I had food poisoning," he continued from a safe distance. "You know, from the school lunch. My mom almost called the principal about it."

"She almost called," Matt repeated.

James nodded solemnly. "That's a serious threat."

Barry paid no attention. He just went on talking. "How come you guys are hanging around out here? The show's about to start. You want to go in? We could sit together."

"No, thanks," James said. "We'll probably leave soon anyway."

"Leave? Without seeing the show? So you aren't allowed to go after all. Then what are you doing here?"

James gritted his teeth. "I'm allowed to go."

"What's the matter, then? Don't you have enough money for a ticket? Personally, I have plenty. I could lend you some."

"We have enough," Matt replied.

Puzzled, Barry scratched his head. Then he smiled. "Oh, now I get it. I bet your parents heard about your science project, didn't they, Matt? So no circus for you. And if you can't go, James won't go either, right? Wait until I tell the guys."

Barry waved at a couple of other sixth-graders. They acted like they didn't see him.

"Hey, wait up!" he called, and he ran off to join them.

"Sorry, Matt," James said. "He shouldn't have said that about your project. It almost worked."

"It doesn't matter. Nobody listens to him anyway. Barry is 'personally' way too annoying these days."

"Yeah, I bet if he only had a minute to text all his friends, he'd still have fifty-nine seconds to spare."

Matt laughed. "Well, at least he's out of the way for now."

James looked around. Everyone else had gone to watch the circus. From inside the tent came the sound of lively music, signaling the show had started.

"Nobody's here. Let's do it," he said.

The lion didn't seem to care when they slid behind its cage. They immediately went to the back of Z'Nia's. Buddy had removed the stuffed gorilla and pushed her cage right into the trees. Most people wouldn't even notice it.

James planned to lift the edge of the tarp to pass the food through the bars. He'd start by cutting one of the ropes. He reached into his pocket and found his knife. Then, from somewhere nearby came the sound of a rasping cough. James froze.

A voice challenged them. "What are you boys doing here?"

The owner of the circus stepped out of the shadows. He glared at James, his hands balled into fists. With uncombed black hair and a three-day-old beard, Slade looked like he'd just climbed out of bed. A stain splashed down the front of his jacket.

As the man moved closer, James detected a sharp, piney scent.

Beer, he thought.

One time last summer, he'd sneaked a few swallows of his dad's beer when no one was looking. He still wasn't sure how much he liked that biting, slightly bitter taste, but he did recognize its distinct scent.

Yep, it's definitely beer, he decided. *Slade's angry, and he's been drinking. Not a good combination.*

The man stepped closer still. His jacket fell open, revealing a handgun tucked into the waistband of his pants.

James had never seen a gun before, not close up. This one looked big and black and threatening. A memory came to him. Gunshots, loud and frightening. Bark splintering from the side of a tree.

Who was shooting? he wondered now.

He couldn't remember. But he knew that in the hands of a bad-tempered man, a man who'd been drinking, a gun could be especially dangerous. He hoped this one wasn't loaded.

Chapter 12

James

"What are you doing here?" Slade asked again.

James took a breath and tried to forget about the gun.

"Bigfoot," he said. "We wanted to see him. Some guys from our school said he's in this cage. They bet we'd be too scared to look."

Slade steadied himself against a tree. "But you're not?"

"No," James said. "He's pretty quiet, not like in the films we've seen on TV. We thought he'd growl a lot or maybe bang on the walls."

Slade's laugh sounded bitter. "This one's not a he. It's a she. And she's pretty tame all right."

"Hey," Matt said. "You mean she's a fake? Is that why the cage is covered up, so no one can see her?"

"No, no, she's the real deal. I bought her from a bunch of hunters who captured her about fifty miles north of here."

"Yeah, sure," James said. "Let's go, Matt. My dad warned us this would be a come-on."

Matt nodded. "I never believed it anyway. Those posters looked phony. You can tell your dad he was right."

They turned to leave, but Slade blocked their path.

"Wait a minute," he said. "You can't go telling people stuff like that. You'll ruin my business."

James moved to walk around him. "Okay, mister, whatever you say."

"I'm serious. Come here. You're going to see bigfoot right now. Give me that knife."

James hesitated. Putting a knife in the hands of this man didn't seem like such a good idea, but refusing might just make him angry. Finally, he handed it over, and Slade sawed at the rope. James and Matt exchanged a thumbs-up behind his back.

James sent Z'Nia a message.

It's Matt and me, he told her. *Slade caught us trying to get into your cage, so we said we wanted to see bigfoot. We'll hand you the food as soon as he's gone.*

She replied, *Be watchful. Do not trust him.*

When the strands of the rope parted, Slade returned the knife and drew back the tarp so the boys could see into the cage. Z'Nia lay against the far wall. James saw the steak Buddy had brought her shoved into the opposite corner.

Slade found a stout tree limb. He poked it through the bars at Z'Nia. But his hands shook, and the branch skidded harmlessly across the floor of the cage.

"Hey!" he shouted. "Hey, bigfoot! How about giving these boys their money's worth?"

Then he laughed. "That's funny. Nobody's paying a cent to see this worthless animal."

He poked at Z'Nia again. This time the stick hit her leg, and she winced.

"Stop it," James said. "Don't hurt her."

The man ignored him.

"I'm the one who needs to get my money's worth," he muttered. "I paid top dollar for this thing, and I aim to see it riled up for once."

He positioned himself to get a better shot and thrust the branch at Z'Nia's head.

"No!" James yelled, pulling at the man's arm.

Z'Nia moved aside, but too slowly. The branch hit her shoulder.

Slade glared at her. "How about that, bigfoot? That make you angry? Come on. Show us what you got."

James grabbed at the branch, but Slade growled and shook him off.

"Get away from me, kid," he said, and he gripped the branch more firmly. "I own that animal, and I can do whatever I like with her."

"No, you can't!" James said.

He tried to get between Slade and the cage.

Just then, Buddy came to investigate the commotion. He took the stick from his boss's hands. Slade was so busy glaring at Z'Nia that he didn't seem to notice.

"What's goin' on here?" Buddy asked. "These boys givin' you trouble?"

James saw Buddy was a big man, well over six feet tall. He had a long face, brown hair and eyes, and a slightly crooked nose. Some injury had left him with a pronounced limp. Dressed in jeans and a plaid shirt, he carried a bucket of water for one of the animals.

Slade gestured toward Z'Nia's cage. "I'm just showing these boys our star attraction. Bigfoot. Supposed to make me rich. That's a laugh!"

He went off toward the parking lot, pausing only to shout at Buddy, "Don't give that animal one more bite of food, you hear me? I'm not spending another cent on her upkeep."

Buddy made a half-hearted salute. "Whatever you say, Boss."

James and Matt pressed up against the bars of the cage, trying to see Z'Nia.

"She hurt?" Buddy asked.

James looked at him. "He hit her really hard with that stick."

"He aimed at her head," Matt said. "I think he wanted to kill her."

Buddy rubbed his chin. "Boss has a mean temper, especially when he's been drinkin' like this."

He spotted something lying in the dirt. Then he leaned over to pick up the bag of food James had brought for Z'Nia.

"What's this?"

"We brought some food," James said. "Just in case we got to see her."

"You brung this? Don't look like somethin' a wild animal would want."

"We heard bigfoot is a vegetarian," James replied.

"That so?" Buddy stared at the boys. At last, he said, "Well, let's see if she likes it."

He grinned as he handed the food to James and Matt. "Boss didn't say you guys couldn't feed her."

James ripped the package open. He took a handful of greens and stretched his arm into the cage, but he couldn't reach near Z'Nia.

"She's hurt, and I can't reach her. Isn't there some way to get closer?" he asked.

Buddy fished in his pocket for the padlock key. "I could get closer, but I'll have to be careful. Any animal, even a tame one, can be pretty fierce when it's in pain."

Buddy unlocked the door, leaving the padlock dangling. Then he took the handful of greens from James and went inside.

"Guess I'll be feedin' her after all," he said. "But at least the boss didn't pay for it."

He advanced a step and held out the food, but he still couldn't reach her. Finally, he tossed it.

"Come on," he said. "These boys brung you somethin' special. You gonna try it?"

Z'Nia opened her eyes and reached for the food. Buddy backed away. He turned to shut the door.

"She's eating," Matt said. "Give her some more."

Buddy went over to get the bag of sprouts.

In a flash, James jumped inside the cage and crossed the floor to kneel beside Z'Nia. When she looked up at him, the memories came flooding back. Here was the face he remembered, but the soft brown eyes were now shadowed by sorrow, the kindly features lined by pain.

Are you hurt bad? he asked.

These wounds will heal. I just need to rest.

You won't get to do that. Slade's going to dump you out along the road, somewhere between here and the next town.

I will be free? She sounded hopeful.

Yes, James said. *But you're not as strong as usual. Won't it be hard for you to survive on your own?*

Perhaps. But it is worth the danger if I can be free.

Please be careful, James told her. *I don't want anything bad to happen to you.*

A sort of gasping sound caught his attention. He looked behind him and saw Buddy standing in the doorway, clutching the door frame for support. His mouth hung open in disbelief.

"Come out of there," Buddy said. "She ain't no pet."

James ignored him and turned back toward Z'Nia. As he watched, she put a leaf into her mouth. She chewed and swallowed it and then reached for more.

Is the food okay? he asked. *We didn't know what you'd like.*

It is just what I needed, she said.

Good, James said. *I'm getting you out of here. I promise.*

She smiled, closed her eyes, and soon went to sleep. Knowing Z'Nia might have trouble with the packaging, James opened the bag and left it on the floor where she could reach it easily when she awoke.

Now he had to get to work on keeping his promise.

CHAPTER 13

James

"Where'd you learn to work with animals?" Buddy asked.

James shrugged. "It's just something I know how to do."

"It's a gift," Matt said.

Buddy mopped his forehead. "I'll say. I'd get fired if the boss heard about you bein' in that cage, though."

"We won't tell him," James said. Talking to Mr. Slade about Z'Nia would be like swatting a hornet. Not much use, and possibly painful.

"Then I won't tell him she got somethin' to eat," Buddy replied.

He closed and locked the cage door. "Course it don't matter whether she eats or not. Boss is gettin' rid of her before we get to Richland. Told me so last night."

"He won't try to hurt her again, will he?" James asked.

Buddy paused. "I can't say what he might do. He's mad 'cause he paid a lot of money for her. At first she struggled, and folks liked to see that, but she's too quiet now. She don't move much. Most of the time, she don't even make a sound."

"She shouldn't be caged up," James said.

"Yeah, I wouldn't want to be in that cage myself, but the boss don't see it that way. He just knows he ain't gettin' his money back. Business bein' what it is, that's all that matters."

"It's not her fault if business is bad," Matt said.

Buddy shook his head. "Times are hard for small operations like ours. Slade's cut costs to the bone."

He laughed. "You should see the stuffed bigfoot that usually sets beside her cage. Looks just like a gorilla. See, Slade didn't want to buy a new figure, and we already had the stuffed gorilla. So we dyed its coat to match hers."

That explains why nobody knows about her, James thought. *People see that moth-eaten gorilla and think it's all a hoax.*

"It's too bad," Buddy went on. "Used to be, Slade loved the circus. Now it's all about the money."

James mimicked his tone. "Yeah, too bad, but you know he's gonna hurt her. We have to do something."

"Calm down," Buddy said. "Tonight, after the crowds are gone, I'll hang around out here just to make sure everything's okay."

"What if he comes back sooner?" James asked. He didn't trust Slade, not one little bit.

Buddy's mouth twisted. "I'll bring her some water during the show. It'll give me an excuse to check on her. That's the best I can do. And if the boss sees me here and orders me to leave, I gotta do it. I can't lose this job."

He pocketed the padlock key. "Now you boys run along and see the show. I've got work to do."

So do I, James thought.

He watched Buddy lift the heavy bucket and limp away, sloshing water with each uneven step.

"What should we do?" Matt asked. "We can't leave her here like this. She's helpless."

"Not as helpless as you think."

"What do you mean? She's just lying there."

"She's tired now," James said. "But once she's had some food, I bet she could walk pretty good. That's all we need her to do."

"Walk? Where's she gonna walk to, James? She's locked up."

"For now."

James studied the padlock on the cage.

"What are you doing?" Matt asked.

"Keep your voice down," James said.

He pulled out his pocket flashlight and gestured at the trees crowding the back of Z'Nia's cage. "Let's take a walk."

Matt followed him into the woods. "Where are we going?"

"I want to show you something."

James led the way. After a while, the woods ended at the edge of a farmer's field.

"There it is," James said. He brushed a leaf from his hair, squinted at it, and then put it in his pocket to save.

He looked out at the field. The farmer had already harvested his crop, leaving only clods of dirt and a scattering of hay bales to be picked up later.

"What am I supposed to see?" Matt asked.

"That's Prescott's land. The Scouts went on a hayride out here a couple of years ago, and we passed an old barn. Remember?"

"Yeah, I see it. So what?"

"That's where we're gonna hide her," James said.

They stared at the dilapidated building. Years of weathering had stripped the color from its siding and rotted out some sections of wood. But though the walls sagged, the metal roof seemed solid. James figured a barn sturdy enough to store farm machinery could shelter Z'Nia for the short while she would need to be there.

Satisfied, he turned back toward the circus.

"Wait a minute," Matt said. "Aren't you forgetting something? She's in a locked cage. How are we gonna get her out?"

"Maybe Buddy would give her to us," James said.

"Right." Matt's voice dripped sarcasm.

"Yeah, that's what I thought, too. So, do you know how to pick a lock?"

"Oh, sure," Matt joked. "I got the lock-picking badge in Cub Scouts, didn't you?"

James grinned. "I have only one other idea."

"What's that?"

"Magic."

"Very funny," Matt said, but he didn't laugh. "Come on, what's your real plan?"

"That is my real plan," James replied. "Last night, I saw some of the signs on the attractions. One of them said something about sleight-of-hand tricks. I guess it stuck in my mind, because I dreamed about a magician making people disappear. And when I woke up, I remembered how magic works."

"You get the audience to look at one thing while you're really doing something else," Matt said.

"Exactly. I'm gonna need your help, though."

"Okay, what do I have to do?"

James reminded Matt that Buddy had promised to bring Z'Nia more water. As soon as the cage door was unlocked, Matt would provide a distraction while James got Z'Nia to go into the woods.

"What kind of distraction?" Matt asked.

"Whatever you want. Can you do it?"

"Sure," Matt said. "I'll think of something."

Then he got serious. "They'll search for her. And Prescott's barn is pretty close. You know that."

"Yeah," James said. "But she won't be there long, just overnight. And then I can help her get back home where she'll be safe."

"Do you have a plan for how to do that? Getting her home, I mean."

"I'm working on it," James said. "I'll tell you later."

He had a couple of ideas but wasn't ready to share them yet. But he had permission to stay at Matt's house again tonight. They'd have time to make plans after the circus.

Matt had one more comment. "If we get caught, Slade will say we're stealing from him. And he's got a gun."

"I know. I saw it. But he's gonna hurt her. We can't just walk away and hope it doesn't happen."

Matt didn't say anything.

Maybe he doesn't want to get involved, James thought. *I can't blame him. After all, Slade's a dangerous guy.*

He felt relieved when Matt finally said, "You're right. So when should we do it?"

James had already thought about that. "Tonight. We're supposed to meet our parents for the second show. We'll say we're going for snacks and come out here instead. Nobody will be around, and there'll be plenty of noise to cover whatever sounds we make."

By that time, they had reached the circus grounds.

This has to work, James thought. *I'm out of ideas.*

Almost out of time, too. The circus crew would pack up after tomorrow's last show and get ready to move on. Before that happened, Z'Nia had to be away from here. As far away as possible. James had to make sure she was beyond Slade's reach.

CHAPTER 14

James

"Wonder what the first act will be," Matt said.

The Braden and Oliver families had found good seats in the tenth row of the bleachers. Though he and Matt claimed the places closest to the aisle, James could feel his mother's gaze on him from a few yards away. Lindsey's, too.

"Don't know," he replied.

James had too much on his mind to think about that. He wanted to get on with freeing Z'Nia. He didn't even care about seeing the performance.

But then the lights dimmed. Despite his concern for Z'Nia, James felt a stir of anticipation. His gaze followed a pair of spotlights sweeping back and forth across the center ring. The lights came to rest on a man in a bright red coat and a top hat.

"Ladies and gentlemen, boys and girls," the ringmaster shouted. "Welcome to Slade's Amazing Circus Escapades!"

At a wave of his hand, the parade commenced. Performers in spangled costumes marched around the ring in time to a recorded tune. The audience clapped along with the music.

James watched a trio of horses prance by, their braided manes trailing bright ribbons. Then a troupe of acrobats cartwheeled across the floor in complicated patterns. Next, a man in a wide-brimmed hat led a pair of llamas, while the baby elephant carried a boy dressed as Aladdin. The parade continued for almost ten minutes, though James suspected some of the performers marched by more than once.

Finally, the ringmaster introduced the first act, and the acrobats tumbled their way into the spotlight. They walked on their hands, turned cartwheels, and did a series of flips. Finally, they created a human pyramid, and the youngest of the group vaulted to the top to do a headstand.

"Wish I could do that," Matt said.

The pyramid broke apart, and the tumblers ran off.

A moment later, two jugglers entered the ring. They set a half dozen torches on fire and began tossing them back and forth. The audience applauded.

Everybody's watching those jugglers. It's time for us to leave, James thought. He nudged Matt.

"We're gonna get some snacks," Matt told his parents.

"We didn't have any dinner," James said.

A food counter stood near one of the exits. The boys purchased bags of buttery popcorn, then joined some classmates who had front-row seats. After a brief conversation, James and Matt squeezed in next to them. They waved to their mothers to show where they'd be sitting.

Minutes later, when the spotlights focused on the jugglers' finale, the crowd stood up and cheered.

"Come on," James said.

He and Matt casually walked over to the food counter, ducked behind it, and then slipped outside. As they'd expected, the area around the big top was deserted. Because all their customers were watching the show, the concession booths had closed for the evening.

James wiped the salt from his lips and tossed the rest of his popcorn into a trash barrel. After stuffing one last handful of corn into his mouth, Matt did the same. Then the boys darted behind the nearest of the booths. Careful to stay in the shadows, they ran silently toward the animal cages.

With the show in progress, most of the cages were empty. A workman inside the dogs' cage was refilling food and water bowls.

"That's not Buddy," Matt whispered.

"Yeah, I know. Guess he has an assistant."

James was actually happy to see someone other than Buddy. As requested, Matt had planned a distraction. He would pretend to be injured and call for help. Now he wouldn't have to disguise his voice.

"I'm gonna move closer," James murmured. "He'll probably do the bear's cage next and then the lion's. Z'Nia's would come after that. When you yell, make it sound good. We don't want him to worry about locking the door before he goes to help you."

Matt gave him a thumbs-up. James slipped around the side of the booth and headed toward Z'Nia's cage.

He immediately sent her a message, asking, *Are you awake?*

James, where are you?

I'm right behind your cage, he told her. *When the guy brings you water,* act like you're asleep. But be ready to move when I tell you. I'm getting you out of there.

I will be ready, she promised.

Then he could do nothing but wait. The workman finished up in the bear's cage and walked off. A few minutes later, he returned with two buckets of water. He set one on the ground and took the other into the lion's cage.

Soon, James heard a clanging noise.

"There, that's done," the man said.

He came out of the cage, closed the door, and twisted the key in the padlock.

"Don't know why Buddy stuck me with this job," the man grumbled. He mimicked Buddy's voice as he said, *"Louie, you do the cages tonight. I don't feel so good."*

He moved the remaining water bucket close to Z'Nia's cage.

"Funny, he looked okay to me," Louie said. "Oh, well, nothing but water for this one."

He opened Z'Nia's cage and went inside, leaving the padlock behind. James could hear him moving around in there.

It won't take him long, James thought.

He inched closer to the door until he could reach up and slide the padlock from its hasp. Then he took a stone he'd found earlier and lobbed it in Matt's direction.

Matt immediately cried out, "Oh, help! Somebody help me!"

The sounds inside Z'Nia's cage stopped abruptly.

"You hear something?" Louie asked.

James wondered if he realized he'd just talked to "bigfoot."

"Help!" Matt called out again.

Louie came over and peered out of the doorway. "Hello? Is somebody there?"

"I'm here," Matt called. He'd made his voice sound hoarse. "I need help!"

"Yeah, okay, I'm coming," Louie yelled. He reached around to lock the door, but the padlock had disappeared. "Now where'd that thing go?"

Louie started searching the ground. Only a few feet away, James held his breath.

Matt groaned loudly. "Oh, help me."

Louie hesitated. He glanced back inside the cage.

"She hasn't moved," he muttered. "Probably half-dead anyway. Should be okay."

Go on, Louie, James thought. *Go find him.*

Matt groaned again. "Oh, it hurts!"

Louie closed the door.

"I'm coming. Where are you?"

He hurried off toward the nearest concession booth. Matt's voice had come from that direction, but James knew that Matt had already moved.

His mind called to Z'Nia's. *Now!*

I am coming, she replied.

The door swung open on well-oiled hinges. James held it while Z'Nia climbed down the steps.

Please wait for me in the woods, he told her.

As soon as she had disappeared among the trees, he closed the door and dropped the padlock on the ground near the cage.

James could hear Louie stumbling around in the dark, searching for someone who'd been hurt.

"Man, where you at?" Louie kept asking.

But Matt didn't answer. Before many minutes passed, Louie would give up the search and come back here. James had to go.

Matt's okay, he reassured himself. *He'll meet us in the woods just like he promised. Now all I've gotta do is get Z'Nia away from here before anyone finds out she's gone.*

CHAPTER 15

James

Twenty feet inside the woods, Z'Nia stood waiting for James. She looked up expectantly when he reached her.

Where are they? she asked.

James was confused. *Who? You mean Matt? He's coming in a minute.*

I mean the captive animals. Did you not free them as well?

James had not thought about releasing any of them. He understood Z'Nia's concern, but what could he do? It was too late to change his plan now.

They're not here, he said. *They're working.*

No, the bear is in his pen. The llamas are in their cage, too.

He heard Louie bungling around near Z'Nia's empty cage. Any minute now, the man could discover she was gone and come looking for her. They had to get away from here.

We're coming back for them, he told her. *After we get you safely away, Matt and I will come back. But we need to leave here now.*

Z'Nia stared at him. James struggled to keep his expression blank, but he felt the blood rush to his face. He carefully kept his thoughts to himself.

Very well, she said at last. *We will move on.*

James breathed a sigh of relief and followed her into the woods. He didn't use his flashlight. He couldn't take the chance someone might see its tiny beam. It didn't matter, though. Z'Nia walked among the trees without bumping a single one.

She can see in the dark, he realized.

And she moved as quietly as she'd done years before. Although James tried to copy her silent pace, the fallen leaves rustled softly with his every step.

Z'Nia acted weaker than he'd thought she would. She often put out a hand to steady herself against a tree. He remembered how quick and sure her steps had once been.

That was nine years ago, he reminded himself.

He wondered how long the Tazsmin lived. Maybe he'd expected too much of her. Maybe this was normal behavior for a Tazsmin her age.

Suddenly, Z'Nia sank to her knees and leaned forward, head bowed against a tall oak.

Concerned, James sent her a frantic message. *What's the matter? Is it your shoulder?*

I am fine, she replied. *But this tree is not. Can you not see the damage?*

She caressed the spot where someone had tried to carve his initials onto the bark.

James understood now why Z'Nia had been walking so slowly. All the while, she'd been finding living things that needed her help.

Matt chose that moment to appear. He raised his hand for a high five. James slapped his palm, careful not to make much noise.

"It worked just like you wanted it to," Matt whispered. "That guy searched for at least five minutes."

"But he didn't see you?"

"Nope. He finally went back to the cage and almost tripped on the padlock. Even after he found it, he didn't check inside the cage. He just locked the door and left."

For the first time in hours, James relaxed. A little of his worry drained away.

This might work after all, he thought.

But Matt had been looking around for Z'Nia. Finally he saw her kneeling under the tree.

"What's the matter with her?" Matt asked. "You said she'd be okay."

"She'll be fine. She just needs to rest."

"Maybe," Matt said. "But it's taking too long. Our parents will notice we're gone."

James glanced at his wristwatch. "We've got about ninety minutes until the show ends. Should be enough."

Z'Nia stood up then. She and Matt looked at each other.

Matt's eyes got big. He took a step back. James remembered that his friend had never really seen her before. In the darkness, she appeared even larger than usual. To someone who didn't know her, she would certainly look scary.

James heard Z'Nia's alarm as she asked, *Who is this?*

"It's okay," he whispered. "Z'Nia, this is my friend, Matt. He's nervous because he doesn't know you, but he'd never hurt you. And Matt, she's scared because of what humans have done to her. But, trust me, she'd never hurt anyone."

73

Both Matt and Z'Nia still seemed wary. Trying to make them more comfortable, James positioned himself between the two of them. He gestured in the direction of Prescott's field.

"Let's get moving. Matt, how about we let Z'Nia go first? She has night vision."

So on they went. Even though James urged Z'Nia to keep going, she made frequent stops to tend the sick or injured plants she found along the way. They were nearing their destination when she sank to the ground once more.

"Hey, is she okay? She doesn't look so good," Matt said.

James hadn't told Matt about Z'Nia's healing ability, and he didn't know how his friend would react. She must have seemed scary enough without any extraordinary powers. He decided Matt better not see what she was doing. At least not yet.

So he gave Matt his flashlight. "She needs to rest again, just for a minute. The field's right over there." He pointed. "Can you check to make sure everything's okay? Once Z'Nia's on her feet again, I want to get her into that barn."

Matt went off, but James knew he wouldn't be gone long.

"Hurry!" he whispered.

She looked at him with reproach and let him know that healing should not be rushed.

Then she turned her full attention to the brittle needles on a pine tree. She sang softly about love and peace. In only minutes, the needles seemed more flexible.

Before James could comment, however, Matt had returned.

"We got a problem," he said.

"What do you mean?"

"There's somebody out there near the barn. I could see his cigarette, shining in the darkness."

James went cold. "Slade?"

"I couldn't tell," Matt replied. "Might be Farmer Prescott for all I know."

"But why would anybody be out there now? It's too dark to work, and besides, that field is already harvested."

"Beats me. The thing is, we can't get to the barn until he leaves. What are we gonna do?"

That, James thought, was an excellent question.

CHAPTER 16

James

They stood at the edge of the woods. Clouds covered the moon, leaving the earth in darkness. A hulking black shadow showed the barn's location, but James could see no one near it. He heard nothing except the rustle of dry leaves trembling in the wind.

"Maybe he's gone," James whispered.

Matt pointed out the spark of light.

"There, see? I don't get it. First we can see the light, and then it disappears. A few seconds later, it's back again. What's he doing?"

James could only guess. "Maybe pacing back and forth? I can't tell if it's Slade, can you?"

Matt shook his head. "Nope."

Z'Nia sent the answer to James. *It is Buddy.*

You're sure? James asked her.

It is his scent.

James trusted her judgment. He knew all her senses were much keener than his own.

"It's Buddy," he told Matt, forgetting his friend didn't know about his mind-link with Z'Nia.

"How can you tell?" Matt asked.

James thought fast. "It's the way he moves. See how the light kind of bobs up and down? That's how Buddy walks."

Once he said this, he knew it was true.

"Oh, yeah," Matt said. "You're right."

"But why is he here?" James asked. "And why now? Why would he tell Louie he was sick and then come out here to stand around outside this old barn?"

He remembered Z'Nia's comment about Buddy being kind but not brave. Could he have suspected what they were doing? Could he be here to help them? Even if he was, could they trust him?

James made a decision. "We need to find out why he's here. I'm gonna go ask him."

"Wait a minute. Why not both of us?"

"Because we can't risk both of us getting caught if this turns out to be a set-up. Somebody has to be ready to go for help. That'll be you."

"No way. I'll go talk to Buddy, and you can stay with Z'Nia."

James shook his head. He wouldn't let his friend take the chance of walking into a trap.

"It's my idea, Matt. I'm going."

James couldn't see Matt's face in the darkness, but he could picture the flinty eyes, the stubborn set to the jaw that always signaled his friend's displeasure. Matt never wanted to be left out of the action.

I need to let him know how much I appreciate everything he's done, James realized.

He said, "I didn't get a chance to tell you what a great job you did back there at the circus. You sure fooled that guy Louie. You'd have fooled me, too, if I wasn't in on the plan."

Matt forced out a grudging, "Thanks."

James went on. "If it wasn't for you, Z'Nia would still be in that cage. But if anybody's gonna take chances now, it has to be me. You gotta let me handle this myself. Okay?"

There was no answer.

"Okay, Matt?"

"Yeah, okay."

Quickly, James told Z'Nia that Matt didn't know about their mental communications.

Can you hear me from that distance? he asked silently.

She said she could.

Then if I tell you to hide, you have to do it. Agreed?

She hesitated. *I agree.*

"Matt will be here if you need help," he said aloud. "Z'Nia, please do whatever he says."

Matt muttered some reply that sounded irritable.

James struck off across the field, aiming for Buddy's lighted cigarette. He moved as quickly as he could over the uneven ground. As he walked, the moon slid out from behind a cloud to light his path. He knew it would also let Buddy see him, but he didn't care. He had a feeling Buddy was expecting him anyway.

The cigarette stopped moving. James could see a dark silhouette against the moon-silvered barn siding.

When he drew near it, he heard a voice ask, "Who's there?"

"I bet you already know who it is, Buddy. What are you doing here?"

"I could ask you the same thing."

"I asked you first," James said.

Buddy stepped out of the shadows, and James saw his troubled face. His mouth pulled down at the corners. Worry lines etched his forehead and chiseled deep grooves beside his nose.

"I overheard you and your friend talkin' about bigfoot earlier, about how you was gonna get her out tonight and hide her in this barn."

"I'm sorry if it causes a problem for you," James said. "But you know why we had to do it."

"Yeah, I know. That's why I sent Louie to do the cages tonight. He's not real smart. I figured he'd fall for whatever 'distraction' you and your friend cooked up."

"He did. Thanks."

Buddy's lips stretched into a crooked smile. "I didn't want you to get caught."

"Then you wanted her to escape?"

"Yeah, I guess I did."

Buddy threw his cigarette to the ground and stepped on it.

"But then why are you here?" James asked again.

"Because Slade plans to kill her. He says he's gonna do it after the show tonight. He's drunk and angry, but I think he means it. In a couple hours, he's gonna be lookin' for her."

"Can't you stop him?"

"If I tried, he could shoot me, too. Same with you. I remember one time Louie forgot to feed the elephant. Boss got mad and took a shot at him. He missed, but Louie learned not to cross Mr. Slade. You gotta learn that lesson, too, or you might get hurt."

"But if she's gone—" James began.

Buddy shook his head. "He'll search for her. Might not start till the sun comes up, but he will search. And if she's here, this close to the circus, he'll find her. And then he'll— Well, I can't be sure what he'll do. I just know it won't be good."

He started to walk away, but James stopped him before he'd taken more than a couple of steps.

"What do you think we should do?" James asked.

Buddy turned back to face him.

"I can't help you with that," he said. "But one thing I know. You can't leave her in this barn. Get her as far away from here as you can. Do it tonight."

CHAPTER 17

James

Buddy headed back toward the circus. James followed in his wake, angling over toward Matt and Z'Nia once he reached the trees. While he walked, he thought about what to do next. He didn't come up with much.

"He came to warn us," James said. "Slade's threatened to kill Z'Nia tonight. Buddy thinks he'll find her if she's in that barn. We've gotta take her someplace else."

Z'Nia sent him an apology for causing so much trouble.

We'll think of something, James told her silently.

Then he asked Matt, "You got any ideas?"

Matt's face puckered in thought. "There's not much around here. If we go east, we'll come to that new mall they just built."

"So that's out," James said. "What if we go west?"

"There's a road about a mile over. Prescott's farm went all the way to County Line Road until he sold off some land for houses. I heard Mr. Hardin telling my dad about it. There's about a half-dozen houses over there now."

James frowned. "Then we can't go that way, either."

"Should we try the barn anyway?" Matt asked.

"No way. Buddy was serious."

Z'Nia touched his arm. She gestured toward the woods again.

"She thinks she'll be safe here," James told his friend. "But I'm afraid Slade will find her."

Z'Nia pulled at him.

I am not a child, she reminded him. *I can take care of myself.*

I know, he replied. *I'm sorry. It's just, that guy Slade is evil.*

But he could think of no other solution.

"Okay," James said at last. "I guess the woods is our only choice. But let's at least get away from the circus."

They decided to go west, where there would be far less traffic than near the mall. To avoid being seen, they walked just inside the trees. Though Z'Nia moved more slowly than James would have liked, she did increase her pace.

Fifteen minutes later, they had put as much distance as possible between themselves and the circus. The woods ended fifty yards away at County Line Road. Strung along that length of blacktop, due west from Prescott's barn, stood six identical white ranch houses. Each half-acre lot had a fenced-in backyard with a couple of shade trees and a shed. Just beyond the fence line, harvested fields stretched all the way back to that old barn.

"We're awful close to those houses," Matt whispered.

"I know," James replied. "But it's probably safer than near the circus."

While Matt went to check out the housing development, James sent a message to Z'Nia. *Are you okay here, so near to humans?*

I know how to stay hidden.

She paused and pointed toward the north. *I could make my way home. My cave lies in that direction.*

No, James protested. *It isn't safe. Not with all the hunters around here. Besides, there are more fields than forests in this area, and you're not strong enough to go very far tonight. Somebody would spot you for sure, and then you'd be locked up again. Or worse. Promise you won't do that.*

She thought about it. *I do not understand the world of humans, so I may need your help to get home. So I will give you my promise, James. For now.*

Matt returned and said everything seemed quiet on County Line Road. James told him they would leave Z'Nia here. He pulled out the last bag of greens from the Thrifty Check, opened it, and put it into her hands.

He spoke aloud so Matt could hear. "I know you can find your own food, but you need to rest. I'll come see you tomorrow and we'll figure out how to get you home."

And then they left. To save time, the boys stepped outside the trees and ran across the fields until they reached Prescott's barn. When they started back through the woods, James heard far-off music playing. The volume increased as their pounding footsteps brought them nearer. Soon, he saw the crowd pouring from the big top. The show had ended.

"We made it," he said.

Winded from the run, Matt didn't reply.

James wiped his face on his sleeve and waited for his breathing to slow down. Then he neatened his hair and beat the dust from his jeans.

"There's a thing on your jacket," Matt said.

"A thing?"

"You know, one of those helicopter things from the maple trees."

James found the seed pod clinging to his left shoulder. He ran his thumb across its surface, then put it away to study later.

"Ready?" he asked.

"Yeah," Matt said.

The boys merged into the crowd and moved toward the entrance to the big top. As they pushed through a group of their classmates, they heard bits of conversation.

"I liked the dogs," one girl said. "They were so cute."

"Don't forget the monkeys," her friend replied. "And what about those guys on the trampoline? They were awesome."

Just ahead, James could see his family waiting with Matt's mom and dad.

"Where could they have gone?" Mrs. Braden asked. "They knew we'd look for them after the show."

"We're right here," James said, and she whirled to face him. "We were with those kids over there."

She looked over his shoulder, but the other sixth-graders had moved on. "Oh, well, I'm glad you're here now. What did you think of the show?"

"We liked it," James said. "Especially the jugglers. Dad, do you think I could learn to do that?"

His father grinned and shook his head.

Matt chimed in. "Everybody liked the dogs … and the monkeys."

"Don't forget the trampoline," James said.

The adults smiled at their enthusiasm, but Mrs. Braden seemed vaguely uneasy. James noted the little vertical lines between her eyebrows that appeared when something bothered her.

What's worrying Mom? he wondered. *Have I got leaves in my hair or something?*

He furtively ran a hand across his head but found nothing unusual. His mother didn't seem to notice.

She said, "James, why don't you come home with us? Tomorrow morning, we're going to carve the pumpkins for the front porch. You don't want to miss that, do you? And I'm going to bake some of those oatmeal cookies you like. You know, the ones with the pecans and raisins."

James understood her underlying message. His mother didn't like him spending a second night away from home. He didn't want to upset her, but he and Matt needed time to talk.

"I'm sorry to miss doing the pumpkins, Mom. But Matt and I already made plans. You said I could stay over. Remember?"

Her smile tightened in a way that told him she wasn't happy.

"Maybe you could save me some cookies," James said.

"We'll see," she replied, her voice cool.

Then she relented. "Of course I'll save you some cookies. I know they're your favorites. And Josh's."

"That's what worries me," James said. "He'll eat my share, too."

Everyone laughed. Then they all moved toward the parking lot. James and Matt trailed behind and waited while Matt's dad loaded their bikes into the back of his van.

"It's bed for you two when we get home," Mrs. Oliver ordered. "And I don't want to hear any argument."

James didn't think he'd get much sleep anyway, not with Z'Nia in danger. Would Slade wait until tomorrow to go after her, or would he decide to kill her tonight? And could Buddy be trusted not to give them away?

Matt must have learned mind-reading in one of those concession booths. As they climbed into the backseat, he muttered, "Don't worry. She'll be okay."

"Hope you're right," James said, but the thought of that big, black gun left him feeling cold. "I really hope you're right."

ΩΩ   ΩΩ   ΩΩ

Lindsey

Lindsey paused by the car door, watching James.

He's dead tired, she thought.

Both James and Matt had flushed faces and damp hair. If she didn't know they'd been at the circus, she'd think he and Matt had been out running.

The thought came out of nowhere: *Running scared.*

That's ridiculous, Lindsey told herself. But she couldn't ignore the goosebumps that suddenly lined her arms.

She'd lost sight of James at the circus tonight. One minute, she could see the back of his dark head, right there, a half-dozen rows below her. And the next minute, she couldn't find him.

But the lighting was bad. The tent was crowded. There were lots of other dark-haired boys.

I made a mistake, that's all, she'd thought.

Lindsey had forced herself to watch the show. She'd even flirted a little bit with that cute guy sitting next to her. But although she'd reminded herself that James no longer needed a babysitter, she couldn't help feeling anxious. Her eyes kept looking for him. Pretty soon, that cute guy had sensed he didn't have her full attention and started talking to another girl instead.

Darn it, there I go again, letting James ruin everything, she'd thought. She'd looked down at her fingernails, perfect ovals painted with "Daring Coral" polish. A waste of time.

When she'd entered high school last year, Lindsey had decided to give up watching over James. She thought she'd been obsessing about him long enough. And though she'd had a few relapses, she did manage to cut back on playing the guardian angel role. She'd started to relax, have some fun, even joined the choir.

Now, in just one evening, all her protective instincts had reawakened. In fact, they were on high alert. Her father would say she was obsessing again.

I'm not, she thought defensively. She preferred to think of herself as "careful." No, better yet, "attentive."

Besides, it's probably nothing. Who understands boys anyway? Maybe they got all sweaty racing across the parking lot.

But a sense of dread filled her, reminding her of the time she'd forgotten to study for an exam. Had she missed something important tonight?

She argued with herself, *James is twelve now, almost a teenager.*

But teenagers get in trouble, too, she thought.

Lindsey decided not to say anything to her parents. After all, she wasn't a snitch. Besides, she didn't want to worry them if this turned out to be nothing. But she would talk to James about it at the first opportunity. Somehow, she'd get him to tell her what was going on. She had to find out why he'd looked so scared.

CHAPTER 18

James

The next morning, James and Matt got up before the sun rose and headed downstairs for breakfast. Mrs. Oliver set out bowls and spoons, boxes of cereal, cartons of juice and milk.

"You guys help yourselves," she said. "What are you doing today? Didn't you have some project to work on?"

Matt poured out a serving of Fruit Krispies and passed the box to James. "We're training for the school Olympics."

"Isn't it kind of early? They aren't held until May."

"Yeah, but it'll be winter soon, and we won't be able to ride our bikes. We want to do at least fifteen miles today."

His mother smiled. "Sounds like you're determined. Will you be back for lunch?"

"Probably not. We'll pack something just in case."

"I'll do that for you," she said.

"No, thanks, we can do it," Matt replied.

Mrs. Oliver looked surprised. "Okay, if you want to."

After she left the room, they loaded their backpacks with sandwiches and chips, fresh cookies that smelled of cinnamon, and cans of their favorite soda. Then they added several bottles of water for Z'Nia, plus some cabbage and raw green beans.

"I bet she'll like this stuff," James said.

"Better her than me," Matt replied.

James grinned. He dug into the Fruit Krispies box for a last handful of the grape-flavored cereal.

The phone rang.

"Can you get that?" Mrs. Oliver called. "I'm loading the washer."

Matt picked up the phone. "Hello?"

He listened to the voice on the other end.

"It's for me," he shouted to his mother. And he whispered to James, "It's Barry McAfee."

James stopped eating the cereal.

Matt told Barry, "I don't know anything about that."

A minute later, he said, "Wait, I'm pretty sure that's private property."

He paused to listen again. "No, we didn't. That's not true. Barry!"

Matt put the phone down. "He hung up."

"What did he want?" James asked.

"He saw us running across the field last night when we went back to the circus. Turns out Barry's family moved to County Line Road last summer."

"You're kidding."

"Wish I were," Matt said. "Anyway, he asked why we were out there after dark. I tried to act dumb about it, but he insisted he saw us. He's going over to the woods."

"We've gotta get out there," James said. "If he saw Z'Nia, he'd call the police … or some TV news crew!"

The boys pulled on their jackets and said good-bye to Matt's mom.

Outside, a clear, cold morning awaited them. The wind had blown last night's clouds away and left everything glazed with a sparkling frost. James barely noticed. He'd worried through the night about someone finding Z'Nia. Now his fears had come true.

They rode straight to County Line Road, right past the row of look-alike houses. The name on the fourth mailbox said "McAfee."

"Should we stop to talk to Barry?" Matt asked.

Before James could answer, the door opened, and a woman stepped outside. She marched down the driveway and stopped directly in front of them. Eyes narrowed, mouth pinched tight, she looked furious.

"Matt Oliver, I remember you. And that's James Braden, isn't it?" she asked.

What's this about? James wondered.

The boys looked at each other apprehensively.

She didn't even wait for an answer to her question. "Barry said you two were responsible. And I think this is the worst trick I've ever heard of. I'm going to call your parents."

"Wait, Mrs. McAfee," James said. "We don't know what you're talking about."

"I don't believe you," she said. "Barry saw you in the woods this morning."

"But we just got here."

Matt echoed the denial.

"You're lying," the woman said. "You led Barry to that patch of poison ivy and pushed him into it. He took a shower right away, but his rash just seems to be getting worse."

Now James understood. "So Barry found some poison ivy in the woods today?"

"You know he did. You made sure of that."

"Really, we didn't," Matt said.

But she wouldn't listen to them, just went back into the house. Not until the echo of the slamming door died away did the boys get back on their bikes and ride off. James looked over his shoulder and saw Barry's mother watching them through the front window.

"You think she believed us?" Matt asked.

"I doubt it."

"She won't call our parents," Matt said. "She just likes to make threats."

"Yeah. I bet you're right."

But James wondered what would happen if she did call. He knew his parents would listen to his side of the story, but it would be hard to defend himself without mentioning Z'Nia.

"Why'd Barry have to involve us in this?" he asked. "He got into that poison ivy without our help."

Matt shrugged. "That's Barry. No matter what happens, he always blames somebody else. It's like that time he dropped his lunch in the cafeteria. He said it was Sara Zimmer's fault, and I know she was at least six feet away from him. She had to help clean up the mess, though. For some reason, grown-ups seem to believe whatever Barry says."

"Well, this time he's gonna pay the price all by himself," James said. "And he deserves it. He shouldn't have spied on us. I'm just glad he didn't see Z'Nia, or his mom would be yelling about that, too."

"Yeah, that's lucky," Matt said.

But James still worried. Though Z'Nia had probably managed to avoid contact with Barry, she might have gone back toward the circus. Not too near, he hoped.

"We can't go find her now," he said at last. "Not while Barry's mom could be watching."

"Let's come back later," Matt said.

Once out of sight of the McAfees' windows, the boys stopped at a roadside park and sat on a weathered picnic table.

Matt took out a can of soda. "I figured we'd have problems today, but I didn't expect this."

He flipped another can to James. James popped the top, and soda sprayed everywhere.

"Wonder how Barry really found that poison ivy," Matt said. "Maybe he saw Z'Nia, started running, and tripped over his own feet."

James wiped his sticky palms on his jeans. "I don't think she'd let him see her."

"But maybe she couldn't help it."

James drained his soda can, crushed it against the table, and lobbed it into a trash barrel. Then he said, "She'd hear him coming and get out of there."

"You think she went home on her own?"

"Not in broad daylight," James replied. "But she might move to a different part of the woods. She knows how to hide."

"How do we find her again?"

James tried to imagine what Z'Nia might do, where she might go to avoid Barry.

"Guess we'll have to walk through the woods until she finds us," he said.

They rode back to the woods and locked their bikes to a tree. Hoping Z'Nia hadn't gone far, they decided to start where they'd last seen her. They called her name softly, but she didn't respond. After searching for an hour without any luck, they finally sat under a tree to rest.

"Good thing you left her some food last night," Matt said.

"She'll need more than that to build up her strength," James replied. "But mostly, I'm worried about finding her before someone else does."

"Okay. Where should we look?"

James started to answer, then paused to listen. He heard the voices of at least two people, and one of them had a raspy cough.

"It sounds like Slade," he whispered. "We can't let him see us."

They quickly pushed behind a cluster of evergreen trees. James found if he stooped a little, he could look between two branches. A moment later, he saw Buddy and Slade enter the clearing.

"There's no sign of her anywhere," Slade said.

"Why don't you give up?" Buddy asked. He turned to face his boss. "Admit it. She's probably long gone by now."

"Not unless she had help. She's not strong enough."

"Maybe not."

"And," Slade continued, "I'm still trying to figure out how she escaped from that cage."

"Yes, sir, that's a good question."

"I'm holding you responsible, Buddy."

"Yes, sir."

James felt guilty.

Buddy's in a spot because of us, he thought.

"I pay you to take care of the animals," Slade said. "Somehow you managed to lose this one. How could that happen?"

"I don't know, sir."

"Don't interrupt me!"

"Sorry, Boss."

Slade hadn't finished. "I paid twenty thousand dollars for that animal. Twenty thousand! Money I was supposed to get back from all the people who'd want to see her."

"But you planned to get rid of her anyway."

"I said don't interrupt!"

"Yes, sir."

Slade began pacing back and forth. The longer he paced, the madder he looked.

If he sees Z'Nia, he'll kill her for sure, James thought.

"Theft," Slade muttered. "That's my animal, and it's gone. Somebody has to pay for that."

He turned on Buddy. "You let her escape. You got any idea how long it would take you to pay back twenty thousand dollars?"

"A long time," Buddy said.

"A very long time. If I took fifty dollars out of your paycheck every month, you'd still be working it off when you're an old man."

Slade frowned. "I can't wait that long."

"No, sir."

Slade paced some more, slashing at the bushes in his anger.

"I need that money," he said. "Somebody would buy the pelt, I bet. It's a nice color. Cleaned up, it would look pretty good. You know, not everybody has a bigfoot rug in front of the fireplace."

"Not everybody would want one," Buddy pointed out.

"I don't need everybody. I just need one person who wants something nobody else has. Think I can find one person like that?"

Buddy's answer sounded reluctant. "Probably."

"I think so, too," Slade said.

His smile reminded James of a snake.

"I'm gonna get my property back," he continued. "I talked to a farmer this morning, and I'm gonna call him right now. He's got some tracking dogs."

Dogs! James nearly cried out. Matt's expression mirrored his own alarm.

Slade pulled out his cell phone and stalked away.

"Hutchins? I've decided I want your dogs after all. Yeah, I'll bring the money. Fifteen minutes."

Buddy stood there for a minute, scuffing one boot at the dirt. Finally, he turned and trailed after his boss. He looked very unhappy.

CHAPTER 19

James

As soon as Buddy's footsteps died away, the boys scrambled out from behind the trees.

"He's gonna get dogs!" James whispered.

James had never gone hunting, but he had read books about it. He'd seen movies and heard classmates telling stories. He knew dogs could hunt down an animal, and when their owners allowed it, some dogs would viciously attack.

"We've gotta find her," Matt said.

But where could she be? They had already covered the most likely areas and couldn't search the rest of the woods in such a short time.

"You sure she wouldn't just take off?" Matt asked.

"Positive," James replied. "We must have missed her. Let's check close to the road again."

Back they went, searching for any clue as to where Z'Nia might be. After what seemed like a long time, James heard her voice.

Look up.

He did. Only because she moved did he spot Z'Nia perched high in an oak tree.

What are you doing up there? he asked.

I had to get out of the way. Someone came to the woods this morning.

That was Barry McAfee, James replied. *I know him from school. He's a trouble maker.*

I think he found some trouble. Her amused tone told James she had seen Barry stumble into the poison ivy.

Slade and Buddy were here, he told her.

Yes, I heard much of their conversation.

Slade's bringing dogs.

Yes, James, I know.

The dogs might hurt you. Even if they don't, Slade probably will.

I will be fine, she said. *But you and Matt are in danger. Slade will suspect you helped me escape.*

James thought about it. Would Slade remember them from the previous evening? Probably.

He felt Matt pulling his arm and realized he'd been standing motionless for several minutes.

"Hey," Matt said. "You're in a trance again. Are we gonna look for her or not?"

"I found her."

James pointed upward, and Z'Nia waved one arm.

Matt grinned. "Wish I could climb that high. How do we get her down?"

"We don't. She's safer up there than down here. With luck, they won't even see her."

From far off came the barking of dogs that had found a scent. James heard two sounds, an excited yip and a long mournful howl. The dogs must be tracking Z'Nia.

"Let's get out of here," he said.

The boys hid in a tangle of brush not far from Z'Nia's oak tree.

James heard a message in his head. *Be safe.*

Yeah. You, too, he told her.

The hounds drew nearer. James heard them thrashing through the woods and imagined them straining at their leashes. He heard men's voices, too. They sounded excited that the dogs had so easily picked up a scent.

"Go on now!" an unfamiliar voice urged them. James thought it must be Hutchins.

Slade shouted, "Good dogs! Go get her!"

Then the dogs bounded into view, trailing their leashes. The larger dog was a mixed breed, some kind of hound with a low, full-throated growl. A spotted beagle bounced just behind it. Its high-pitched bark sounded eager.

The dogs sprang at Z'Nia's oak tree and pawed at the trunk.

"Oh, no," Matt whispered. "They're gonna find her!"

Just then, the wind sang from the treetops, though not a leaf had stirred. The dogs froze, ears held high to listen, until the sound died away. Only James knew it was Z'Nia, singing about love and peace.

When Slade and Hutchins arrived a moment later, they found the dogs sniffing happily at a rabbit hole.

"What's going on?" Slade asked.

"Guess they lost the scent," Hutchins replied. "Give 'em a few minutes to try again."

But the dogs started playing, rolling in the grass and licking each other's faces. They showed no interest in tracking.

"I want my money back," Slade said.

Hutchins slowly pulled out a roll of bills. He peeled off several of them and offered them to Slade.

"All of it!"

Frowning, Hutchins handed over the rest. Then he grabbed the leashes and hauled his dogs away into the woods.

"Can't depend on anybody these days," Slade said.

He slammed his fist against a tree. Then he pulled the gun from his waistband, aimed at a fallen log, and … *bang!* Bits of wood flew everywhere.

"Gonna get something today," he muttered.

He looked around, apparently searching for a better target.

Wide-eyed, James and Matt flattened themselves onto the ground. *Bang!*

"Missed," Slade said a moment later. "Didn't want a squirrel anyway. I'll get a goose instead."

They heard another *bang* and then more grumbling.

"Must be something wrong with this gun. Can't hit a thing!"

The boys heard him trampling the undergrowth as he went back toward the circus. Relieved, they lifted their heads.

"We've gotta get Z'Nia out of here," James whispered. "What if he comes back?"

"Can you get her to come down?"

"I don't know. I'll see."

Cautiously, James went over to the oak tree. He softly called out to Z'Nia, asking if she could come down.

I am not strong enough just now. And I must wait for nightfall or take the chance of being seen. There is no better place to hide.

All right, he replied. *I'll be in trouble with my mom if I don't get home for dinner. I'll come back after dark.*

"She won't come down," he told Matt. "Can't blame her. She's pretty well hidden where she is."

"What're you gonna do?"

"Go home for dinner. My mom's expecting me, and she won't be happy if I'm late. I'll leave the food and water for Z'Nia. Then tonight, after the last show, I'll come back to get her. I'm taking her home."

The boys found their bikes and rode off together. James was vaguely aware of Matt talking about a Halloween prank a couple of their classmates were planning. It had something to do with Brittany Barnes and a fake tarantula. James pretended to listen. He even muttered responses from time to time, like, "Sure. Uh-huh. Great idea, Matt." But he wasn't really paying attention.

Taking her home. It sounds so easy, he thought. But he knew it wouldn't be.

He replayed Z'Nia's message in his head. She'd said she wasn't strong enough.

What did that mean? Would she be able to climb down from that tree? He hoped so, because he couldn't think of any way to help her with that. And if she did get down, would she be able to move quickly?

Dusk would fall in about four hours. He'd have to wait even longer before he could sneak out and come back for her. He hoped she could gather her strength by then. Tonight, she'd need it.

CHAPTER 20

James

Hours later, James returned to County Line Road. He braked to a stop, his bike tires sliding across the blacktop. There wasn't a scrap of moon or a single star to reveal his presence. An owl hooted, away in the distance. It made him feel lonely. He hoped the McAfees were sleeping too soundly to hear that owl … or him.

James dismounted and adjusted the straps of his backpack. He wheeled his bike into the shadows edging the woods and left it there, not even bothering to lock it up. He was late.

First, he'd had to wait for his parents to go to sleep. Then, some animal had overturned a trash can and roused the neighborhood. James had finally sneaked out but lost precious minutes waiting for unexpected traffic to clear the downtown. By the time he got moving again, the rain had started, forcing him to ride slowly or risk skidding off the road.

I'd better hurry, he thought.

James swiped one jacket sleeve across his face to dry the rain and clear his vision. He decided he'd need his tiny flashlight to guide him through the trees.

He knew he'd find Z'Nia. He had a connection to her, a sort of radar beam showing him her location. He visualized a path. Left. Right. Around a big clump of pine trees and then right again. And at the end, she'd be waiting.

James set off quickly, his footsteps beating a soft, steady cadence across the fallen leaves. The cold mist had finally lifted, but the wind had grown stronger. It knifed through his jacket, and he turned up his collar against the chill.

He hoped Z'Nia was warm and dry. He hoped she'd found the food and water he'd left near the oak tree.

Suddenly, James stopped short. He had a strong impression of Z'Nia trying to reach him, but the message had no words. It was pure emotion. Fear? Pain? He couldn't tell.

Something's wrong, he thought. He started running.

Minutes later, he spotted a lofty oak tree. He bent down and put out one hand to touch it. Yes, this was the tree Z'Nia had climbed that morning. Around its base, he could feel the marks made by the dogs' frantic clawing. He couldn't see Z'Nia, though.

His mind asked, *Where are you?*

The answer came slowly. *Here. Behind you.*

James closed his eyes and pictured her, curled beneath the spreading limbs of an ancient pine. He stepped away from the oak, angled south, and reached her in seconds. When his flashlight lit her face, her skin looked damp and a little gray.

Are you all right? he asked her silently.

Adequate, she replied.

He played the beam across her fur. Why did it look so sticky? Was that blood?

Did you hurt yourself when you climbed down?

She paused a moment. *No. The gun—*

James remembered the loud gunfire, Slade's bullets biting deep into the tree trunks. One of them must have creased her shoulder.

Slade shot you, James said. He knew she could hear his anger.

She grimaced. *He aimed at a squirrel and hit me instead. It is not life-threatening. Merely painful.*

Can you heal it?

No, I cannot heal myself, only others.

James wondered how much blood she'd lost. If she'd been wounded critically, would she even let him know? Or would she try to hide it from him?

Can you walk? he asked.

If necessary.

It is. I'm taking you home.

Z'Nia smiled. *I would like that very much. When can we go?*

We've gotta go now, he said. *Let me help you.*

She gave him her left hand, sparing her wounded right shoulder.

Silently, he communicated his plan to her. They'd have to go back to the circus grounds.

Z'Nia shook her head.

It's the only way, he said. *And we've gotta do it now while there's still time.*

I do not want to be anywhere near Slade.

I know, he replied. *But it's our best chance. Trust me.*

Finally, she agreed.

Even with help, Z'Nia walked slowly. James fretted at their pace, which seemed little better than a crawl. He remembered how easily she'd carried him years ago, how swiftly she'd run through the forest. Would she regain that strength and quickness?

I hope so, he thought, but he was careful not to share his concerns with Z'Nia.

Mostly, he worried about being late. If only that trash can hadn't made so much noise. If only it hadn't rained.

Z'Nia sensed he wanted to hurry.

I can go faster, she told him, and she did.

Soon, James saw light filtering through the trees. He heard familiar noises. Beside him, Z'Nia tensed with fear. James felt scared, too, but he knew no other way to get her home.

He left her resting against a tree and ran ahead to see what was happening. Light and noise meant humans were around, but that didn't worry him. In fact, James had expected it.

In a moment, he returned and sent her a mental picture of what he'd seen: lined-up trucks, their engines running while men stacked equipment inside the trailers. Part of Slade's fleet of circus transport, the trucks waited at the east end of the lot, near the roadway.

Must we do this? she asked.

It's the only way I can think of to help you get home.

They moved forward, carefully, quietly. The sound of the motors grew louder, and the scent of diesel fuel invaded the forest. Soon, they neared the east edge of the woods and peered out from beneath the trees.

Just in front of James and Z'Nia sat three large trucks, two of them already closed up. A work crew loaded equipment into the third. Its open doors faced away from the road, and James could see a hodgepodge of cargo inside. Tent poles, lumber, and lengths of canvas lay in one messy pile. Beside the fun-house mirror stood the stuffed gorilla, wearing a wide-brimmed feathered hat. Beaded costumes, coils of rope, and striped popcorn bags spilled onto the floor.

The crew's in a rush, James thought. *They don't have time to pack things carefully.*

He checked his watch and saw it was 5:43. Matt's dad had heard from Mr. Hardin that the circus must leave this lot by 6:00 AM, so he and Z'Nia needed to get on that truck in the next few minutes.

Wait here, he told her.

Careful to stay out of sight, James ran back about fifty yards. He unzipped his backpack and pulled out a remote control Jeep. Ten inches high, it had fat off-road tires that could easily run over the uneven ground. The string of firecrackers attached to it had an extra long fuse.

James positioned the toy to face the vacant lot, well clear of trees and brush that might catch fire. After he checked the remote control battery, he carefully lit the fuse the way he'd seen his dad do it the previous summer. He crushed the match into the dirt and ran back to Z'Nia.

Get ready, he said.

James turned on the remote control and pushed the lever. The truck moved out into the lot. No one noticed it. But seconds later, the firecrackers began to crackle loudly. *Bang! Bang-bang!*

One of the workmen said, "Uh-oh, I thought we already packed those fireworks."

He and the rest of the crew ran off in the direction of the remote control car.

Let's go, James told Z'Nia.

He steadied her while she climbed into the back of the trailer, then scrambled in after her. He surveyed the cargo, trying to find a place to hide.

Under the canvas, he said.

She ducked, and he pulled the red fabric over her. When he heard voices from outside the truck, he dove behind the fun-house mirror.

He made it just in time. The work crew had returned, and they began loading a stack of boxes.

"Just a prank," one of the men said. "Everywhere we go, there's one or two of 'em."

Another man chuckled. "Sure had me fooled. I thought some idiot set off the fireworks left over from last night."

James let his breath out a little at a time. The diversion had worked just as he'd planned.

But despite his relief, he couldn't help wondering if their luck would hold.

What's gonna happen when we stop in the next town? he worried. *What's gonna happen when it's time to get off this truck?*

CHAPTER 21

James

Thud! Something heavy hit the floor.

Just outside, one of the crewmen said, "That's the last of it. We better get moving. We have to set up in Richland for a Monday night show."

Fifty miles northeast of Tyler's Ferry, Richland was not far from his family's old picnic site. James thought Z'Nia had a shelter somewhere near there.

"Relax," another of the workers replied. "The other trucks are already gone. We'll make it."

James heard the crunch of gravel as footsteps approached.

Then came Slade's raspy growl, "Did you pack those boxes like I told you?"

"Yeah, Boss, everything's packed just like you said," one of the men replied.

But Slade wouldn't take his word for it.

"Give me that roll of tape. I want to see for myself," he said. "You guys stay here."

James heard the scrape of boots climbing onto the truck and knew Slade was coming on board. He peeked cautiously around the edge of the fun-house mirror to make sure the canvas covered Z'Nia.

You're completely hidden, he told her.

Then he noticed the stack of sealed cartons piled between her and the truck's back doors. Could those be the boxes Slade wanted to check? He'd be standing right next to her.

I am fine, Z'Nia said. *You also must remain still.*

James listened to the hollow-sounding footsteps that crossed the floor and stopped just feet away. A small gap between the mirror and its supporting framework allowed him to see Slade. The man had shaved that morning and combed his hair, and he wore fresh clothing. Still, James smelled alcohol again.

Beer for breakfast, he thought. He stifled a laugh. *Wonder what Rachel's mom would think about starting the day with beer.*

97

Slade surveyed the stack of cartons. He pulled one down and shook it, producing a soft swishing sound.

"That's not it," he said.

He quickly pushed the box aside and grabbed a second one.

Rip! This time he removed the tape from the carton, and again, James heard his raspy voice.

"This one looks okay, too. Can't believe those boneheads got something right."

Watching him reseal the second box, James thought, *Slade must be paranoid or something. He's checking every carton.*

Already, Slade had pulled down a third box. It rattled.

"That was supposed to be on the bottom," Slade said, his voice tight with anger. "It says 'Private' right on the lid. How could they miss that? I told them, 'Bury that box under the others.' But do they listen? No. I gotta do everything myself."

James heard the box hit the floor. It didn't sound heavy. He wondered what it held that was so important.

"Better check it just in case," Slade muttered. He knelt on the floor, one knee brushing the canvas that hid Z'Nia.

James held his breath.

Careful, he's right beside you, he told her.

But Slade showed no interest in the canvas. He tore the sealing tape from the box and opened the cardboard flaps.

"Hey, Boss!" a voice called from outside.

Slade raised his head. "What is it?"

"That guy Hardin just pulled up. He keeps checkin' his watch. Remember, we have to be off this lot by 6:00 AM, or you'll have to pay for another day."

"Okay, get the other trucks moving. I'll be out in a minute."

Footsteps crunched away, and James heard the order for the other trucks to leave. Meanwhile, Slade pawed through the contents of his mysterious box.

"I guess it's all here," he said to himself. "I gotta hide this stuff. Not in my car, though."

He stretched out his hand to grab the tape but pulled it back hastily as if something had frightened him. James saw a spider crawling across the roll of tape. Could that be what had scared Slade? No more than half an inch across, the spider didn't seem particularly scary. Slade found a popcorn bag and used it to brush the spider away. It fell on the floor and crawled toward James.

Too bad it's not bigger, he thought. *Then maybe it would scare Slade away from Z'Nia.*

A voice called out again. "Hey, Mr. Slade! Hardin has the police out here, and they're all watchin' the clock. We got three minutes."

"Okay, okay!"

Slade looked around, muttering under his breath. "Police! Just what I need! I gotta get this box out of sight. Maybe under the canvas."

He started to lift one edge of the red fabric.

No! James thought, knowing he had to distract Slade somehow.

Impulsively, he nudged the frame of the fun-house mirror. The movement caught Slade's attention. He recoiled. Eyes wide, he stared at the mirror. He stepped backward so quickly that he nearly fell, then stood frozen in place.

Finally, he let out a nervous laugh. "Could be the same spider. It just looks bigger because of the mirror."

Surprised, James realized the tiny spider had been magnified because of the mirror's angle.

Slade still seemed scared. He reached out toward the canvas but pulled his hand back at the last second. It took three tries before he mustered the courage to shove the unsealed box beneath one edge of the canvas. Then he hurried away, his footsteps echoing across the floor.

The doors slammed shut, and James and Z'Nia were left in the dark. He waited to hear the lock engage before he turned on his flashlight.

"Move it out!" Slade yelled.

The truck's motor rumbled loudly. They bumped across the parking area and onto the roadway. Soon, the huge tires hummed along Old Highway 187.

Z'Nia's voice filled James's mind. *Your plan worked. We are on our way.*

He walked over and lifted the canvas. His flashlight shone on Z'Nia's face. Beads of perspiration glistened on her forehead.

Are you okay? he asked.

I am fine.

He pulled the canvas back. *We can relax for a while, at least until we get to Richland.*

He sat down next to her, closed his eyes, and took a slow, calming breath. It was Sunday morning, 6:00 AM. Mom usually let him sleep late on Sundays.

I probably have at least four hours before anyone notices I'm gone, he thought. *Maybe more.*

He hoped that would be enough.

CHAPTER 22

James

The journey to Richland would take little more than an hour.

Not much time at all, James thought.

He fished a crumpled map from his pocket. A crow's feather, a dried oak leaf, and a maple-tree whirligig spilled out with it.

"Sorry," he muttered. "I collect things."

So do I, Z'Nia said.

James spread the map across his knees. His tiny light made a soft glow in the darkness.

"This drawing shows where we are and helps us get where we want to go," he said. He spoke aloud, ready to hear his own voice after so many hours of mental communication.

Z'Nia leaned closer to see the map.

My mother used drawings like these to show the locations of trees or plants that needed care, Z'Nia told him.

His light paused on a red X. "Tyler's Ferry is here. That's where I live with my family."

Yes, I see it.

The light followed a black line, what James knew as "Highway 187," and stopped over a second red X.

"This town is where my dad grew up," James said. "Richland."

Where this truck is going?

"Yes, and here—" He moved the light a little way up the page to find a third X. "This is where I got lost when I was little, when you found me near the hollow in the hills."

When you found me, she corrected him.

James grinned. He still remembered that day. Even as a young child, he'd somehow known that he and Z'Nia shared a secret. And so, he'd followed her.

"When I found you," he agreed. Then he drew her attention back to the map. "But I don't know where your cave is. Can you tell me how to find it?"

She remained silent for so long that James wondered if she'd understood his request.

I promised my mother I would never tell anyone how to find our home, she said at last.

"I'll keep your secret, Z'Nia."

She smiled and said, *Of all humans, I do trust you, James. I will try to show you.*

Her index finger found that third X once more. Z'Nia had never explained why she'd taken him in the first place. Now she described her panicky flight through the forest.

I ran toward the sun's place of rising, she said. *I ran a long way, perhaps a half day's walk for you.*

James felt dismayed.

There's no way she can manage that distance, weak and wounded as she is, he thought. *Not even if I help her.*

But Z'Nia had not yet finished her story. *Finally, I discovered what I had done. I knew I must find shelter for you. So I turned back toward my home.*

James remembered that she'd had several shelters. However, the one she considered to be her home was the cave behind the waterfall.

She continued, *I did not want to take you behind the waterfall. But when I reached the river, it was already in flood stage. I could not cross safely. The cave was my only choice.*

The river? He had only a vague memory of it. James checked the map and found a thin blue line angling from northeast to southwest. It stood for the Cambria River. Less than half an inch above the dot representing Richland, the line made a sharp bend. It showed the river flowing south for several miles before angling west again. That bend would be a good point of reference. He showed it to Z'Nia.

"This line stands for the river. Do you know a place where it turns like that?"

Yes, she said. *The river makes a sharp bend near my waterfall.*

"I can't believe it," James said. "The Boy Scouts found me miles away from there. My parents kept asking me how I walked so far."

Z'Nia smiled. *I am sorry. I could not risk so young a child having information about how to find me. I decided to take you far away from my home.*

"I promised I wouldn't tell."

And you had good intentions. But you were a child, a very young child, and I did not know you well. I do trust the young man you have become.

James thought he understood.

"I wouldn't have trusted a three-year-old kid, either," he said. "But I did keep your secret for nine years."

He hesitated.

I guessed you would have told Matt something, she said. *He is a good friend to you … and to me as well.*

"Yeah, he is," James said. "I didn't mention the waterfall or the mind-link, though. And he doesn't know about your healing powers."

That is good.

"He'll tell my family, too," James said. "I couldn't let you go alone, and I couldn't be here with you unless he told them where I'd gone. You don't know how they worried when I disappeared."

I do know, she replied. *It was in my ninth summer that my mother disappeared for two days. I feared for her. When she returned to the cave, she was dying, shot by a hunter.*

"That's horrible!" James tried to imagine how frightened she must have been, but he couldn't. His own life was safe. Normal.

That is how I learned to fear humans, Z'Nia said.

"Until you met me."

Yes, she said, and her mind-link sounded weary. *But, James, most humans I have met are not like you. I trust only you and Matt, and perhaps Buddy.*

James assured Z'Nia that the Braden and Oliver families could be trusted.

"Matt swore not to tell anyone else," he said. "And he'll make them all promise to keep your secret."

Z'Nia did not reply. James saw that her eyes were closed, her lips slightly parted. Exhausted, she had fallen asleep. Maybe that walk through the woods had tired her more than she'd let on.

I should let her get some rest, he thought. He realized he was pretty worn out, too.

Last night, for the third night in a row, he'd slept for only a few hours. Ever since he'd read that "bigfoot" flier, he had pushed himself to think, to act, to stay alert. Now, his energy seemed to be draining away. He felt like a car with an old battery. It might be running, but no one could predict how long it would last.

James slumped against the side of the truck, wanting to relax for just a minute. He did not intend to go to sleep, only to rest his eyes. But the truck rocked him gently, and the tires played a soothing rhythm against the highway.

The next thing he knew, he was watching the circus again. This time Z'Nia stood in the center ring. Slade entered, gun in hand. He aimed it at Z'Nia. His finger tightened on the trigger. The audience waited, breathless with anticipation, to witness his marksmanship.

Something rattled.

James's eyes flew wide open. He caught sight of a light beam angling beside him.

It's my flashlight, he realized.

It had fallen from his fingers and rolled away. He grabbed it and redirected the beam until it rested on Z'Nia. Slade and his gun were nowhere in sight.

Relieved, James wondered, *How long was I asleep?*

Probably not long, he decided.

His head felt thick, wooden. A dull ache was building behind his eyes.

But something had awakened him, a strange rattling sound. He stretched his legs and heard the sound again as his foot bumped the carton Slade had pushed beneath the canvas.

"What's in there anyway?" James muttered.

He inched the carton nearer to him. Slade hadn't had time to reseal the flaps, so James aimed his flashlight down inside the box. The light caught a gleam of gold, something that sparkled.

"What is all this stuff?"

James wanted to get a closer look. He reached into the box and pulled out a sample of the contents. Suddenly, he understood all too well why Slade had hidden it, why he didn't even want to have this box in his car. What was in this box could mean big trouble for Slade. But James knew it would mean trouble for him and Z'Nia, too.

The desire to sleep left him abruptly. He was wide awake and aware of being in danger.

What do we do now? he thought.

With a hiss of brakes, the truck slowed down and turned left onto a bumpy surface. Gravel crunched beneath the tires. Moments later, the truck jerked to a stop, its brakes squealing a loud protest.

James checked his watch again and saw it was seven o'clock. He put out a hand and shook Z'Nia awake.

"We've got a problem," he said.

CHAPTER 23

Lindsey

At 7:00 AM, the Braden home was quiet. Only Lindsey lay awake, thinking. She often did that.

Just outside her window, a tree limb scratched the siding. The wind rattled a loose board Dad had been meaning to fix.

Could be a storm coming, she thought.

Lindsey hated the very idea of more rain. She usually loved autumn, but not this year. Day after day, clouds had filled the sky, spawning thunderstorms and dulling the bright fall colors. The gloomy weather reminded her of the time James had disappeared.

"As if I needed any more reminders," she murmured.

She frequently dreamed about those days. When she was a young child, she'd accepted the bad dreams as punishment for her failure to keep James safe. Later, she understood dreams could be related to what she'd done or thought about during the previous day. Whenever she felt concerned about James, she dreamed about him disappearing again.

Last night's dream had been terrible. In her dream, James went into his room, closed the door, and vanished.

Lindsey had awakened in a panic, clutching the sheets with tight fists. She'd pulled in slow, deep breaths, her mind filled with the image of James running across the parking lot to join the family.

She shivered, wishing she'd had a glass of warm milk before bed. Regina had suggested warm milk when Lindsey had trouble sleeping the night before a big test. And it worked, at least where exams were concerned. But this was different. This was about James.

Lindsey remembered how tired he'd looked Friday night after the circus. She remembered the expression on his face, too. Something had worried him, and she still hadn't talked to him about it. But today was Sunday. He'd be home all day.

She didn't want to admit she'd been postponing what would surely be a difficult conversation. But she wouldn't wait another day. The only problem was figuring out how to get James to talk to her. He'd think she was intruding. Again.

I don't want to pry, she thought. *But how can I avoid it? He disappeared in the middle of the circus and came back looking scared. I can't just ignore that, can I?*

No, she couldn't. But since there was nothing she could do about it now, she wrenched her thoughts away from James and focused on the upcoming harvest dance. Regina already had a date. Lindsey pictured herself at the dance, sitting alone on the sidelines while everyone else moved to the music.

My social life will be dead if I don't stop worrying about James, she scolded herself. *I'll just take care of this one issue today, and then I can concentrate on other things.*

Bzzzzt! Lindsey heard the sound through the wall adjoining her brother's room. It seemed James had forgotten to reset his alarm.

He must have been really tired last night, she thought. *Too tired to remember that he could sleep late today.*

The irritating sound went on and on—*bzzzzt! bzzzzt! bzzzzt!*

Why doesn't he at least hit the snooze button? she wondered.

She knew the alarm would wake no one else in the family. Mom and Dad's room was at the other end of the hallway, and Josh could sleep through a train wreck. Maybe James could, too.

Two minutes passed, then three.

Annoyed, Lindsey pushed the covers back and grabbed her robe from the foot of the bed. Not bothering with slippers, she padded out into the hallway.

She tiptoed over to James's room. A sign taped on the door said, "Please knock." He'd put that up a few months ago.

On account of me, Lindsey thought.

She knew the sign was his way of telling her to keep her distance. It made her feel guilty, but not guilty enough to stop checking up on him.

She tapped lightly on the door. "James, wake up."

She heard no reply.

"Come on, James. Turn off your alarm."

He didn't answer.

Lindsey pushed the door open a crack and squinted through the gap, but she couldn't see James. She opened the door wider and looked again. She still couldn't see him. No longer trying to be quiet, she crossed the room and stared at the empty bed. When she touched the green comforter, it felt cool. James had been up for a while.

She hurried downstairs and made a quick tour of the house, but she found no sign of him. Then she glanced into the garage and saw his empty bike rack.

Oh, no, she thought. *Not again.*

Back upstairs she ran, this time to pound on her parents' door.

"Mom! Dad! James is missing!"

Lindsey knew she wouldn't be having that conversation with James today. She'd waited too long.

෨෮   ෨෮   ෨෮

Barry

"Hello? Hello, this is Matt. Is anybody there?"

Barry McAfee didn't answer. He'd just phoned Matt Oliver. As soon as he heard Matt say his name, Barry hung up.

"So he is home," Barry said to himself.

Disappointed, he pocketed his cell phone and flopped down on his bed. He'd been so sure Matt wouldn't answer.

Come on, he thought. *Where else would he be at 7:00 AM? He's too lazy to be out of bed so early. And anyway, he did sound like he just woke up. But I could have sworn I saw his Jeep this morning.*

Always early risers, Barry and his parents had driven over to the vacant lot that morning to watch the circus pack up and leave town. They parked across the road, out of the way, near a half-dozen other cars. Dad leaned against the trunk, talking to a couple of men he knew. Mom found someone to gossip with. Except for a baby asleep in its car seat, Barry saw no other kids. So he just watched the circus crew.

Nothing exciting happened until a series of loud *pops* drew all the workers away from the trucks. Barry ran across the deserted highway to find out what was going on. He was disappointed to see only a string of firecrackers tied to a kid's toy. Once the noise had stopped, he'd gone close enough to identify the remote control vehicle that had gotten everyone's attention.

Now he said to himself, *That sure looked like Matt's Jeep.*

He got down on the floor and rooted beneath his bed. He found a jumble of old toys, unused sports equipment, and a few mismatched socks. He had to lie flat and stretch his arm all the way under the bed to grasp what he wanted.

Finally, he pulled out a dust-covered Jeep. He had no doubt at all. The remote control vehicle he'd seen at the circus matched the one he now held in his hand. Back in third grade, he and Matt had bought them on the same day.

In those days, Barry and Matt had been best friends. They had spent lots of time together. When they decided they wanted to try remote control cars, they'd badgered their dads to take them to Straightaway, the local RC store. They had picked out those identical Jeeps, the only two of that model in the store.

For about a month, they'd worked on their Jeeps every weekend. They had even customized them with tiny bumper stickers Barry had made using one of his mom's scrap-booking gadgets. The stickers had said "Best Buddies" in green-and-white script.

I forgot about that, Barry thought.

He rubbed his thumb over a tacky spot on the rear bumper of his Jeep. He'd ripped off his sticker after James Braden joined the Cub Scouts and became Matt's new best friend in the space of a single afternoon.

Barry remembered that afternoon so well. He and Matt had planned to work on their Jeeps after the Scout meeting.

But Matt had said, *I'm gonna ride home with James. I'll see you on Saturday instead.*

Angry, Barry had told him not to bother. He'd watched Matt walk off with James. When Mom came to pick him up, he had tried to act as if he didn't care, but she'd caught him blinking the tears away.

You're better off without that Matt Oliver, his mother had said, her voice fierce with emotion that matched his own. *He's not worth your time, Barry.*

Now, irritated by the memory, Barry shoved the RC vehicle back under his bed. He didn't need to see it anymore.

"That was Matt's Jeep," he said.

But if Matt wanted it back, he would have needed to wait for everyone to leave the circus grounds so he could retrieve it.

I saw somebody chuck it in the trash, Barry thought. *And it was still there when we left for home.*

His parents had stood around talking until after 6:30. All that time, Barry had kept an eye on the trash barrel, watching for Matt to sneak out of the woods and reclaim his toy. But that didn't happen.

Barry pursed his lips in thought. Matt loved that Jeep. Just last week, he'd been talking about repainting it. He'd never let it be trashed like that, not unless he had a really good reason.

Matt could've gone back for it after we left, but he wouldn't have made it home before seven, Barry concluded.

He pictured the route Matt would have had to take.

Nope, he thought. *There's no way Matt could have ridden his bike all the way across town and got home before I called.*

The question remained, if Matt wasn't responsible for that prank, who else could it be?

Barry checked his watch. It was twenty-five minutes past seven.

"Let's see if James is home," he said. Then he called the number.

Chapter 24

James

We've got a problem, James told Z'Nia. He was using the mind-link again now that the truck had stopped.

Instantly alert, she asked, *What is it?*

James described what he'd found in Slade's box.

He's stealing from his customers. Mr. Hardin's gold ring is in that carton. There's a bunch of other jewelry, too, and plastic things called credit cards that are used like money. They have names on them, names of people I know. Slade shouldn't have them.

This is bad?

Very bad.

James had planned to reveal himself as a stowaway once they'd arrived in Richland. He'd planned to apologize to Slade and insist on calling his parents. The diversion would give Z'Nia time to slip away and head for her cave. He'd hoped she could make it alone.

Now I can't do that, he told her. *The minute those doors open, Slade will want to grab that box before anyone sees what's in it. He'll spot you for sure.*

James had to come up with another plan, and he had to do it quickly. Just outside, someone was shouting orders. He heard metal doors slamming open and what sounded like men unloading trucks.

I'll think of something, he said. *We might have a little time. This was the last truck loaded in Tyler's Ferry so maybe it'll be the last one emptied here. Just be ready to hide if we hear someone coming.*

He dug through his backpack to find some food and water. He passed a bag of raw carrots to Z'Nia and unwrapped a peanut butter sandwich he'd packed for himself. While they ate, he thought.

He often solved a problem more easily when he wasn't trying so hard. He'd go to sleep and let his mind work on it overnight. Then, in the morning, he'd have a solution.

Like my dream about the magician, he thought.

But he couldn't go to sleep now, not when those doors might open at any minute. He and Z'Nia could have a conversation, though. Maybe another part of his brain would tackle the problem while they talked.

I want to hear about your life, he told her. *We might not have another chance.*

Z'Nia seemed pleased. She told him about the Tazsmin, how they cared for the earth, and how her ancestors had died at the hands of humans.

Humans attacked your species? Why would they do that? James asked.

They do not understand us, Z'Nia said. *Some humans attack out of fear. Others hope to profit by capturing or even killing us.*

You mean like Slade?

She paused. *I am not sure of his motive. He wants money, but he also seems to enjoy conflict.*

James thought she was right. One time, years ago, Brad Holland had blackened the eye of a boy who refused to hand over his lunch. Kids who would hurt someone for a pudding cup might fight for other things when they grew up. They might even be like Slade.

He shook his head. *How did they capture you? You never let anyone see you. Except for me, of course.*

That comment earned him a smile. But Z'Nia's smile faded as she described how she'd been trapped by hunters.

I saw you at the hollow, she began. *You and your parents.*

You were there? I thought I heard a voice that day.

Yes, that was me, she said. *I forgot to pay attention and found myself surrounded.*

James felt awful. The men had surprised her because she'd been watching him instead of concentrating on her own safety.

I'm sorry, he said.

I knew the danger, yet I was careless, Z'Nia replied. *And lonely.*

She looked away.

But why didn't you fight them? he asked. *Why did you let them take you?*

I had made a choice, she said. *You see, even the Tazsmin were not always so advanced. Centuries ago, they fought and killed, just as other species do now. I do not know why they made the decision to forsake such uncivilized behavior. I only know that they did.*

James nodded that he understood.

Z'Nia went on, *I had to make that same choice when I approached adulthood. I used meditation to help me crush the angry urges I felt. I think my healing powers would have faded if I had not done so.*

And now you can't defend yourself? James asked.

The temptation is always there, she said. *I nearly gave into it when the hunters attacked me. Fortunately, I could not harness my anger quickly enough.*

Fortunately?

Yes, she said, her tone serious. *I would not want to hurt another living being.*

And that's why you didn't escape?

Her smile looked weary. *I could not hurt someone just to be free. At first I did try to find a way out of my prison, but Buddy was very careful. He never left the cage unlocked. Not once. And after awhile, I gave up hope. I thought I had lost my freedom forever.*

Thunk! Something banged against the side of the truck. James tensed, waiting for the doors to open.

"Watch out there!" a voice yelled. "You morons want to ruin one of our best concessions?"

A couple of workers must have bumped the truck while maneuvering the poles used to build the concession tents.

James heard a muffled comment followed by rough laughter. The workers moved away again, and he slowly relaxed. But something they'd said had started his mind working.

Concessions, he thought. *That's where I got the idea about using the principles of magic. I'm fresh out of diversions, though. I need a different idea.*

He put his brain back to work and resumed their conversation.

I'm glad you're free now, he said.

I owe you thanks for that, she said. *Matt, too. My greatest fear was that I would die in that cage.*

James sent her a questioning look.

Z'Nia explained, *The Tazsmin practice certain death rituals. Yet there are no remaining Tazsmin in this part of the world, perhaps anywhere in the world. My one hope is to rest in my own home where I once performed that ceremony for my mother.*

She described the rituals. James thought she sounded sad, as if she wished someone would say those prayers for her.

I'd help if I could, he said.

She smiled. *Thank you, but I have made preparations. When my death approaches, I will recite the prayers myself. It will comfort me to be near my mother. Even though she no longer lives, we maintain a slight connection, a sort of echo of the mind-link we once shared. I can imagine her saying the prayers with me.*

A loud *clang* made James swallow his reply. He froze, listening.

"Watch out!" someone yelled.

"Can't help it," another voice complained. "These trucks are parked too close together. It's like a maze."

James registered the comment and wondered why it bothered him. Again, the work crew moved on.

I'm tired of waiting, he thought. *Now that we're here, I want to get on with it.*

Unfortunately, he hadn't thought of a new plan for getting Z'Nia off the truck without anyone seeing her. All the while they'd been talking, his brain had searched for a solution, but nothing had come to mind. Hoping to spark some idea, he shone his flashlight around the truck's interior.

Suddenly, it hit him. Those locked doors at the back of the truck were the only way out.

It's just like that concession booth, he thought. *The one with the rats in the maze. They managed to find the food okay, but no matter what they did, they couldn't get out.*

This truck was a trap. Z'Nia had seen that. She didn't want to come with him, but he'd insisted. James couldn't believe she still had faith in him. She had to know they were in big trouble.

His watch showed it was already 8:30. Time was running short.

I'm sorry, he told Z'Nia. *I think I've made a mistake. Maybe a really big one.*

CHAPTER 25

Lindsey

Lindsey stood at the window, watching for Matt. Her nervous fingers aligned the drapes into perfect pleats. She pulled a tissue from her pocket and wiped a tiny smudge from the glass. Though her shoulders ached with tension, she couldn't relax.

He's gone again, she kept thinking. *James is gone, and I let it happen. I should have made him talk to me last night.*

At exactly 8:30, Mrs. Oliver's car pulled into the driveway.

It didn't take them long, Lindsey thought. Mom had called the Oliver home less than half an hour ago.

"They're here," she told her family.

She went out on the porch and waited, arms folded against the chill morning air. The rest of the family followed.

"Hi," Mrs. Oliver said. She looked at each of the Bradens in turn, her expression puzzled.

She has no idea what's going on, Lindsey thought. Then her eyes narrowed. *But I bet Matt does.*

Matt wouldn't meet anyone's gaze. He walked past Lindsey to enter the house. When the door thumped closed behind him, he startled like a child caught stealing cookies.

What's got him so jumpy? Lindsey wondered.

"Sit down," Dad said. He, too, was watching Matt.

Mrs. Oliver steered Matt toward the couch and sat next to him. His expression showed that he'd rather be anywhere but here. The Bradens all remained standing, staring down at him.

"Do you know where James is?" Dad asked.

Matt swallowed. "Not exactly."

"But you know something?"

"Yeah, I do. James didn't want you to worry. He asked me to come here and talk to you but not until ten o'clock."

"Please, Matt. You need to tell us now," Mom said.

"I will," he replied. "James told me what to say, but if you want to hear it, you have to promise to keep his secret."

That comment caused an uproar. Everyone started talking at once.

Matt raised his voice to get their attention. "I know you're upset. I told James you would be, but he made me swear I wouldn't tell you anything until you promised."

Josh opened his mouth, but Dad stopped him from speaking.

"We're wasting time," Dad said. "I'll give you my promise. We'll all promise, won't we? Whatever Matt tells us stays right here."

"Yes," Mom said. "Unless it endangers James, of course. But he would know that."

Josh promised, too. So did Mrs. Oliver. Everyone looked at Lindsey.

She didn't like giving her word before she knew what she was promising. But her parents were cautious people. They would have been thinking the same thing, and yet they had agreed to Matt's terms. Besides, Mom had said the deal was off if James's safety was in question. Lindsey decided that would be good enough for her, too.

"I guess so," she said, and they all turned toward Matt.

"All right," Dad said. "Tell us everything."

Tension brought Matt to the edge of his seat. "Okay, here goes. This all started years ago when James was a little kid."

Then he told them the story they'd been waiting nine years to hear.

This can't be true, Lindsey thought. *It's a fantasy. Or maybe he's trying to cover up what's really happening.*

She could see her parents weren't buying this story either. Josh looked skeptical, too. Matt seemed to realize no one believed him. He started over, giving more detail this time.

Oh, sure, Lindsey thought. *What's the real story, Matt?*

But then she remembered how James sang to the flowers, made friends with dogs and cats, talked in his sleep about cavemen.

Cavemen!

Suddenly it all made sense.

"I believe you," she said.

The others stopped listening to Matt.

Josh looked at her like she was crazy. "Come on, Lindsey. You're kidding, right?"

Knowing she had to convince her family, Lindsey shared what she had seen over the years of watching out for James.

"Don't you see? It all fits," she said. "It wasn't a caveman he was dreaming about. It was this creature."

Dad stood, eyes narrowed in thought, for what seemed like a long time. Lindsey watched for his reaction.

"Could be," he said at last.

Then he turned to Matt. "What else can you tell us about the circus owner?"

Matt shrugged. "Slade? He's … I don't know … weird, I guess. I think he drinks." He formed his hand into a make-shift pistol. "And he carries a gun."

Now everyone looked concerned.

"He's not a very good shot," Matt added hastily. But the adults' eyes widened as he described Slade's target practice in the woods.

"Wait," Mrs. Braden said. "We're assuming James actually got on one of those trucks. Maybe he didn't. Maybe he's on his way home right now, and we're worried about nothing."

Matt shook his head. "No. His plan must have worked. Otherwise, he would've called."

"No one's called today except for one of James's classmates," Lindsey said. "And he didn't leave a message."

Dad asked a couple more questions, but Matt had no answers.

"I swear that's all I know," he said. "James planned to call you after he got off the truck. Or if he couldn't call for some reason, he said he'd meet you at your old picnic spot. He said you'd know where that is."

A chill ran down Lindsey's spine.

Back to where it all began. It has to be true, she thought.

For a long moment, the Bradens stared at each other as if unable to move. And then they all grabbed their coats and ran for the car. Matt and his mother watched from the porch.

Lindsey looked at them through the rear window as the car pulled away. She thought Matt still looked worried, but she didn't have much time to think about it. They were headed for Richland and the hollow in the hills.

ଔଠ   ଔଠ   ଔଠ

Barry

At 8:30, Barry McAfee was scratching the poison ivy rash on his left arm and plotting revenge. After a day of unbearable itching, he'd finally gotten some relief with a do-it-yourself remedy his mom found on the Internet. However, the unsightly rash still covered his arms and hands, and the vinegary smell of the homemade ointment drove him crazy.

"It's James Braden's fault," he muttered. "Matt Oliver's, too. They think they're so special, trying to keep their stupid secret from me. Well, I'll show them."

James had to have been responsible for that prank out at the circus grounds. After all, Matt wouldn't have lent his stuff to just anybody, but he'd have made an exception for James.

Besides, when Barry called the Braden home, his sister had said that James was asleep. But Barry had heard lots of commotion in the background. It sounded like a crowd of people talking. Nobody could have slept through that. Nope, James was gone.

There's gotta be a way to use that against him, Barry thought. *He'll be sorry he didn't let me in on his little secret. He'll be sorry he made me get this rash.*

But Barry wasn't really thinking about poison ivy at all. He blamed James for ruining his friendship with Matt, and his anger had been building for a long time. Now he finally saw a chance to get even, provided he got some help from his mom and dad. He put his plan into action over breakfast.

"Something's going on," he told his parents. "Matt's careful about that Jeep. He wouldn't leave it out there in the trash."

His father dug into his ham and eggs. "Maybe so, but I don't see what that's got to do with us. Why is it our problem?"

"Because they're up to something," Mrs. McAfee said. "Matt Oliver and that Braden boy were responsible for Barry getting in the poison ivy."

Barry scratched his nose even though it didn't itch. "Yeah, Dad, maybe I can catch them at it this time."

"Catch them at what?" his father asked, holding out his cup for more coffee.

"Whatever they're doing. I know Matt sacrificed that Jeep for a reason."

"And what would that be?"

Barry paused, unsure what to say. However, his mother had a good imagination, and she disliked James almost as much as he did.

"He probably ran away," she said. "He did it before, you know."

Mr. McAfee's fork stopped moving. "Who?"

"I told you. That Braden boy. He was gone once for three whole days. You should have seen his face when I threatened to call his parents about what he did to Barry."

And Barry knew how to make the truth fit his own purposes.

"James gets in trouble all the time," he said. "Like a couple of days ago, he was chasing a lizard around the science lab. Girls were screaming, the teacher was yelling, and the principal got mad. If Mom called his parents, he'd probably get grounded for life. So he ran away from home. He used Matt's Jeep to get everybody's attention, and then he climbed on one of those trucks."

His dad wasn't convinced yet. He asked his wife, "What did the boy's parents say when you called them?"

Mrs. McAfee's face reddened. "Well, I … I didn't call them after all."

"Then maybe you should," Mr. McAfee said. "We'd certainly want to be notified if someone thought Barry was in trouble."

"All right, I will," she replied.

Barry fidgeted while his mother made the call, but she returned a few minutes later without news. No one had answered the phone at the Braden house.

"You see, Dad? They're out searching for James."

"That's one explanation," his father replied.

"I've never liked that James Braden," his mother said. "I can't imagine what Matt Oliver sees in him."

She caught Barry's eye, and he knew she was thinking about how James had broken up his friendship with Matt.

Excited by the idea of getting revenge on James, Barry and his mom wanted to drive to Richland to "catch him in the act." It took a few minutes of begging—and a lot of scratching on Barry's part—to convince his father to come with them. His dad insisted on finishing his breakfast first, including a third cup of strong, black coffee.

"Okay, let's go," Mr. McAfee finally said. "You two won't give me a moment's peace until we've settled this. And we're only going because we can't reach the Bradens. This is really their business."

As the car pulled out of the drive, Barry could hardly contain his glee over the idea of ruining James's plan, whatever it might be.

"Can we hurry?" he asked. "The circus would have arrived in Richland by seven o'clock."

"I'll drive only as fast as the law allows," his father replied. "We have plenty of time. If the Braden boy is in one of those trucks, he's not going anywhere. It'll take hours to unload them all."

Barry hoped his father was right. He glanced at the bright digital numbers on the dashboard clock.

It's almost 9:00, he thought.

He calculated they wouldn't arrive until about 9:40. He squirmed impatiently, convinced now that James really had hitched a ride with the circus. He could think of no other explanation for Matt's Jeep being at the vacant lot that day.

But why? he asked himself. *Why should James Braden want to get on a circus truck?*

Barry didn't believe for a second that James had run away. Why would he? Describing him as a chronic trouble-maker had been a big stretch of the truth. In fact, James seemed to have few problems with his family. And while he occasionally daydreamed in social studies class, he was one among many. Mrs. Wendell could put anyone to sleep, including Barry.

Well, whatever the reason is, Barry thought, *James is gonna wish he hadn't tried to keep it from me. This time, he's the one who'll be sorry.*

CHAPTER 26

James

James drummed his fingers against his knees. He ran his hands through his hair until it stood on end. Then he looked at his watch for the hundredth time. It was just after 9:30.

They will come soon enough, Z'Nia told him.

He didn't answer.

It's taking too long, he thought. *Maybe Slade knows we're on this truck. Maybe he's waiting to open the door until after everyone else is gone. And maybe he still has that gun.*

A voice from outside interrupted his thoughts. "Okay, somebody get started on that last truck."

James felt relieved. He wanted plenty of witnesses around when he had to face Slade.

Get ready, he told Z'Nia.

They'd hidden themselves again, James behind the fun-house mirror and Z'Nia under the canvas. She hadn't asked him if he'd come up with a new plan. He didn't mention it, either. Not one idea had occurred to him in the past hour. They'd just have to stick with his original program.

When the doors open, you stay hidden, he told her. *I'll make sure they find me. I'll tell them I wanted to run away with the circus, and I changed my mind. Then, when I have everybody's attention, you sneak off the truck.*

Z'Nia didn't like that idea. *Slade is a violent man. Do not put yourself in his hands.*

You're in greater danger than I am, James said. *Don't forget that he's threatened to kill you.*

They silently argued back and forth, James continuing to make his case, and Z'Nia repeating her objections.

Their argument finally ended when the lock disengaged with a *bang.* As the double doors parted, a wedge of pale sunlight spread across the floor. James peeked through the gap in the mirror's frame.

Hey! Maybe we'll be okay, he told Z'Nia. *There's just one guy here. Let's watch for a chance to get off the truck and roll underneath it. And when nobody's looking, you can get away.*

I will try, she said. Then she asked what he could see of the outside world.

James took another look. *I think we're facing north. There's a birch grove not too far away and lots of pines just beyond that.*

I may know where we are, she said. *Do you see a rounded hill with a large boulder at the top?*

About to reply, James heard the creak of the door swinging back on its hinges.

Then Slade yelled out, "Wait a minute. I want to check something before you start."

James felt his hopes evaporating.

He's coming to get that box, he told Z'Nia. *I'll let him see me, and I'll make a lot of noise to attract attention. He'll want to get everyone away from the truck. Once he's done that, you can escape.*

No, Z'Nia said. *I will let him find me while you escape. Slade will not kill me in front of his men.*

And he won't do anything to me when my parents are here, James replied. *I planned to call them later, but I'll do it now.*

As James pulled out his cell phone, he explained its purpose. But then he looked at the display and saw the battery was dead. Sheepishly, he put it away.

Guess I forgot to charge it. I've been kind of busy lately. But don't worry. Somebody will lend me a phone, he said.

Just then he heard a car pull up some distance away, its horn beeping loudly. James thought it might be his parents.

They'd keep Slade busy for a while, he said. *Long enough for you to get out of here. Let me just make sure it's them.*

The crunch of footsteps on gravel told him Slade and his men were walking away from the truck. The doors drifted partially closed. James tiptoed closer to the doorway, intending to peek out. As he did so, he stumbled against Slade's unsealed carton. The box overturned, sending credit cards and jewelry cascading across the floor. Luckily, the commotion outside covered the sound of the spill.

He heard someone shouting. The voice didn't belong to anyone in his family. Yet it sounded familiar.

Wasn't that Mrs. McAfee? And Barry, too? Why were they here?

He peered through the crack between the double doors, but he couldn't see anyone.

Everybody went to talk to Barry and his mom, he told Z'Nia. *We need to get off this truck right now.*

Mindful of that noisy hinge, he eased the door back just enough so he could squeeze through. Once on the ground, he motioned for Z'Nia to follow. Then they slid beneath the truck. James still couldn't see the McAfees, but he could hear them.

Barry said, "I told you. James Braden. He's in my class at school."

Mrs. McAfee added, "He's a runaway. It's your duty to check."

"All right, we'll check," Mr. Slade said. "But first, tell me what you know about all this."

Oh, no, James thought. *I forgot about Slade seeing me a couple of nights ago. If Barry tells him what I look like, Slade will probably make the connection. He's bound to be suspicious.*

He knew he had to get out of there. He had to go with Z'Nia.

What about calling your parents? Z'Nia asked.

James checked his watch.

It's okay, he said. *Matt will be talking to them any minute now. He's gonna tell them to meet me at the hollow.*

He rolled out from under the truck, keeping it between him and the crowd. Z'Nia followed. Bent low, they sprinted for the trees. They darted past the birches and reached the pines without anyone spotting them. There they stopped to catch their breath.

Feeling a cold water droplet on his neck, James realized the rain had started again. He pulled up the hood on his jacket.

Then he parted the pine boughs and looked back toward the road. He could see Barry and his mom, both of them visibly angry. A man who looked a lot like Barry leaned against a tan Honda, letting his family do the talking.

James saw Slade, too, shouting and waving his arms.

What is happening? Z'Nia wanted to know.

Not much. They haven't started searching for me yet.

She leaned down to peer between the branches. James saw her body stiffen.

What's the matter? he asked, worried that her gunshot wound was paining her more than she let on.

She did not reply.

You okay? he asked her.

Z'Nia drew herself to her full height and looked down at him, eyes blazing.

They are still here, she said.

He didn't understand. *You mean Barry and his family?*

I mean the bear cub. The llamas. And all the others. You said you would release them!

James went cold. He'd forgotten all about his promise.

You don't understand, he began.

I understand you did not keep your word. I understand you cannot be trusted.

Stung by her anger, he didn't know how to reply. Finally, he said, *We need to get away from here. Which way?*

She pointed up the hillside and began moving again, using the trees as cover. She did not look at him.

James tried a mental message. *You're doing great.*

But Z'Nia did not reply. She trudged straight ahead, acting as if he didn't exist.

James climbed after her.

It's not fair of her to blame me, he thought. *It wasn't my fault. She doesn't know how hard it was for me and Matt to get her out of that cage. If we'd tried to free all the animals, we'd have been caught for sure. She'd have been caught, too.*

Later, when he had more time, he'd explain it to her. Surely she'd forgive him when she had a clear picture of the whole situation. That's all he needed. A chance to explain.

Convinced he could make Z'Nia understand, James turned his thoughts to Barry. Why was he here? Could this be about the poison ivy? According to Matt, Barry always blamed his problems on others. But coming all this way to get revenge for something James hadn't even done- That just seemed crazy.

He can't separate fact from fiction, James thought. *Well, it doesn't matter anyway. We'll be far away before they even start searching for me. No one will believe that story about me being a runaway.*

And then he remembered. Slade's stolen loot was still scattered across the floor of the truck. He'd know someone had been inside. He'd know someone had seen the evidence.

And he'll know it was me, James thought.

He asked Z'Nia, *Can you go a little faster?*

She looked at him. Though she didn't answer, she seemed to hear the urgency in his voice, and she stepped up the pace.

CHAPTER 27

Lindsey

Lindsey chewed on her thumbnail as she watched the scenery flash by. She realized she'd ruined the polish. She didn't care.

Why is this taking so long? she wondered. *Richland's less than an hour from home.*

But her cell phone showed it was just 9:40. They'd been on the road about fifty minutes. She chewed her thumbnail some more.

Finally, they passed a sign that said, *Richland. 1 mile.*

A minute later, they rounded a curve, and Lindsey saw a fleet of trucks parked in a vacant lot. A crowd had gathered nearby.

"Let's see what's going on," Dad said. "Maybe they found James."

He pulled the car off the road. Across the highway, the circus employees were watching a shouting match involving their boss, a woman, and a boy who appeared to be her son.

"I don't see James," Mom said.

Lindsey didn't see him either. But she did recognize the boy who was arguing with the circus owner.

"That's Barry McAfee," she said.

Josh agreed. "Yeah, and I bet those are his parents. I wonder what they're up to."

Just then, Barry turned and pointed at the Bradens' car.

"If James isn't missing, why are his parents here?" he shouted.

Everyone turned to stare at the black Ford Explorer idling across the road. Barry started toward it, his mother on his heels and his father trailing slowly behind.

Dad lowered the driver's side window.

"Don't tell them anything," Mom whispered.

"Of course not," he said. He turned to greet the McAfees. "Can I help you?"

"Where's James?" Mrs. McAfee asked.

"I don't see how that's any of your business," he replied.

A man shouldered his way in front of the McAfees. "I'm Chet Slade. I own the circus."

"Yes, I know," Dad said. "Is there some problem?"

"These people claim your son broke into one of my trucks so he could run away with the circus."

All the Bradens laughed.

"James? In a circus? That's just silly," Mom said.

"Is he here with you?" Slade asked.

"No," Mr. Braden said. "Again, I don't see how my son is any concern of yours." He gestured toward the McAfees. "Or of theirs. I'm sorry, but we need to be going. We have an appointment."

"Wait a minute," Slade said. He put his hand on the car door.

But Dad raised the window, put the car in gear, and slowly pulled away.

"Looks like they're almost finished unloading," Mom said.

Dad nodded. "And they obviously didn't find James. Since he hasn't called us-"

Mom's head swiveled toward him. "Maybe something happened."

"Let's not jump to conclusions," Dad said. "We'll go on to the hollow like James suggested. It's not far from here."

Lindsey risked a glance over her shoulder. Slade and the McAfees stood in the middle of the road, talking. Barry said something that appeared to capture Slade's interest. The circus owner looked sharply at the Bradens' car, then turned and sprinted toward one of the trucks.

What's up with him? she wondered, mildly concerned.

But Josh was worried about something else. "They could follow us. And we promised James to keep his secret."

"I know," Dad said. He punched some buttons on the dashboard GPS. "Usually I'd take the next left, but I don't want anyone to know where we're going. I'll take a different route."

"Shouldn't we go the fastest way?" Mom asked. "James might be in danger. I want to get up there, Will."

"So do I. But I don't trust those people. Why are they so interested in James anyway? Does he even know them?"

Lindsey replied, "He knows Barry from school. They don't like each other much."

"I can see why," Dad said. "But the one who really worries me is Slade."

Because of the gun, Lindsey thought.

But she didn't say it, and no one else did either, just as no one mentioned the scent of alcohol on Slade's breath.

Her father drove through the intersection, then continued for another mile before turning north. The road took them into Richland. They drove down Main Street, past shops that would not open until after noon. Church-goers walked toward the Methodist Church on one corner. The traffic light there changed to let them cross.

"This detour wasn't such a good idea," Mom said, tapping nervous fingers against the door handle. "Anyone might catch up with us while we're stuck at this light."

Lindsey recognized the edgy tone in her mother's voice.

I feel just the same way, she thought.

After what seemed like hours, the light finally changed. They made it through two intersections before they had to stop again. Dad pulled up behind a line of cars waiting for the light to turn green. Mom kept her eye on the passenger-side mirror.

"Someone's coming," she said. "There's a dark-colored car back there at the last traffic light."

Lindsey turned to see for herself.

"It's probably someone we don't even know," Josh said.

"I bet it's not," Lindsey replied. "Remember what Matt told us."

Dad nodded. "Slade planned to kill that creature. If he thought James had her, he'd follow us to get to James."

"But why?" Josh asked. "He didn't want her anyway."

"That man believes ownership gives him the power to do what he likes. And that makes him dangerous."

"Then I don't want him anywhere near James," Mom said. "What if that's his car back there? What if he follows us?"

Before Dad could answer, the light finally changed. He turned right. After a short distance, he made another right into a used car lot and parked among the other vehicles.

A subterfuge, Lindsey thought, pulling the term from her mental word bank. She'd seen this trick on a movie once and knew their SUV would appear to be one more vehicle for sale.

"Everybody get down," Dad said.

Then he angled the mirror to get a view of the cars passing on the street. A few minutes later, he said they could sit up.

"Was it Slade?" Josh asked.

"It was. He's driving a dark blue Toyota, an older model that's pretty well rusted out. Looked like he was going way over the speed limit. I think he's angry about something."

"And I think we should call the police," Mom said.

Dad looked at her. "Let's go up to the hollow first and see if James is there. I don't want to involve the police yet."

"But, Will—"

"At the first sign of trouble, we'll call them."

Josh spoke up. "We promised James. Right, Dad? Right, Lindsey?"

Lindsey didn't care about that promise. She thought her mom was right. Then she remembered how the Simons once called the police when their daughter was late getting home from the mall. Regina had arrived to find her parents talking to a couple of detectives.

All those questions, Regina had complained. *It's like they suspected me of doing something wrong. It was embarrassing.*

Lindsey knew the police would have questions for James, too. Maybe they'd ask why he'd taken off with an animal that wasn't his. Would that be considered stealing? She wasn't sure.

"We did promise," she began.

"We're not taking a vote," her mother snapped.

"No, we're not," Dad said. "But I'm asking you to do it my way for now, Kate."

Mom shook her head, lips folded tight to hold in her anger. "All right. I just hope we're not sorry."

Lindsey felt impatience growing inside her like a bubble about to burst. With Slade roaming the area, she couldn't stand not knowing where James was.

"Can we go now?" Mom asked.

Dad remained silent as he guided the car out of the dealership.

Mom looked over at him. "I'm sorry, Will. I know you want to find James as much as I do."

And before Slade does, Lindsey thought.

Already she was chewing on her thumbnail again. She had a bad feeling about that man. A really bad feeling.

CHAPTER 28

James

James and Z'Nia had been on the run for almost an hour, up and down hills, over rocky ground, past groves of leafless trees. He had to take two steps for every one of hers. His muscles were starting to ache, and the off-and-on drizzle did nothing to ease his pains. But although he felt cold and wet and tired, he was beginning to feel hopeful, too. They'd finally reached a spot that looked familiar.

We're getting close, he thought.

He followed Z'Nia across a road and up an incline. And then he found himself looking down into the hollow. It looked just the same to him. The meadow was lush and green as ever. Even this late in the fall, a remnant of the wildflower crop still bloomed.

His gaze was drawn to the opposite hilltop. He remembered Z'Nia's bright eyes peering down at him from behind the largest boulder.

Even as a little kid, I knew something important was happening, he thought. *And now, after all these year, we're back here again.*

He saw she had already gone down into the hollow and was waiting for him there. He wondered, was she remembering the day they had met? Or was she thinking about the last time she'd seen this spot, the day she was captured by hunters?

James visualized Z'Nia on her own against four men with guns. She'd been surrounded, unable to escape, and soon overpowered. The image sparked his anger, and it began to grow.

Her mind-link broke into his thoughts. *Is anyone following?*

Grateful she'd started communicating again, James let the disturbing image slide away. His anger went with it. He turned and saw three cars speeding along the road he and Z'Nia had just crossed. A dark older model trailed close behind a tan-colored car. A little way back was a black Ford Explorer like the one his parents owned.

Three cars are coming this way, he told her. *Only my family is supposed to know we're here.*

If you can see them, they might also see you, she reminded him.

So James ran down into the hollow. As always, he appreciated how the gentle slopes rose on all sides, cutting off his view of the world. It gave the place a sense of mystery.

Anything could happen here, and no one would know, he thought.

He noticed Z'Nia seemed tired. She'd worked hard to get this far, but they had traveled only half the distance to the waterfall. Again, he wondered if she'd told him the truth about her injuries.

We should move on, he said. *We don't want to be here if Slade comes.*

She got to her feet and wearily started climbing the incline at the east side of the hollow. James trailed behind her. Though rain had left the hillside slippery, they soon passed the boulders that ran along the hilltop.

This is where you fell when you were a child, Z'Nia said as they scrambled down the rocky slope.

James nodded. His memory of that incident was very faint.

Seconds later, she said she could hear someone coming.

It is Slade, she told James. *And that boy Barry is here with two more adults.*

James wondered how Slade had tracked them. And what was Barry doing here, anyway? But he had no time to guess.

Slade plans to climb to the hollow within the hills, Z'Nia said.

They ran. They reached the grove where Z'Nia had once hidden, but the leafless trees provided scant cover. So on they hurried until they found a clump of pines that would shelter them. By that time, Z'Nia was struggling to breathe.

James suggested they take a rest. He felt mildly alarmed when she didn't argue. He reached into his backpack for the last bottle of water, opened it and passed it to Z'Nia. She gulped it down.

He looked back but couldn't see down into the hollow.

Can you hear them? he asked.

She concentrated. *Slade thinks we must have come this way. He means to search for us. Barry wants to go with him, but his father says he cannot.*

She paused to listen again and then continued. *James, Slade brought the gun.*

James remembered Slade's reckless shooting from the day before. He'd shot Z'Nia by accident, but he'd have killed her if given the chance. He'd certainly do so today if he could get away with it.

You are in danger, too, Z'Nia reminded him. *He will know you were in the truck. He will know what you saw.*

James felt as if someone had squeezed all the air out of his lungs. It was like the time he'd fallen off the end of Matt's front porch and landed hard on his back.

He pulled in a long, slow breath. *My parents are coming. Dad won't let Slade do anything.*

I do not hear any other voices, she replied. *They cannot prevent him from shooting if they are not here.*

James saw she was right.

Then we'll just have to keep going and stay ahead of Slade, he said.

He looked around to get his bearings. The land sloped gently upward for about a hundred yards. Widely-spaced clumps of maple saplings and young pines would provide only a little cover. However, once he and Z'Nia crossed the ridge line, they would find dense woodland. The land would level out, too, which should be easier for Z'Nia to handle.

James pointed. *We need to get up there.*

They alternated several short bursts of running with pauses to catch their breath whenever they reached a clump of pine trees. Each time they stopped, James looked back, but he saw no sign of anyone following them. Finally, they neared the top of the hill.

James estimated the remaining distance. *We've got maybe another fifty feet to go. But there's not much cover.*

I must try, Z'Nia told him.

Both of us. We'll go together.

No, Z'Nia said. *I must go on alone from here. You should be safe from Slade if you stay out of sight.*

What do you mean? I'm coming, too.

Z'Nia shook her head. *I am sorry, James. You have shown me I cannot trust you. Taking you to my waterfall is out of the question now. Perhaps my mother was right about humans after all.*

She started up the hill.

Trust me? he thought. *She thinks she can't trust me?*

"Hey," he said aloud. "Are you still mad about those animals? It's not fair of you to judge me like that. If you'd just listen—"

She paused to look back at him. *It is past time for listening, James. I have learned to value actions above words. You say one thing, but you do another. That is true of so many members of your species.*

"Wait a minute," he interrupted. "I'm not just part of a 'species.' I'm your friend."

I wish that were true, she said. *But you and I have different beliefs. We Tazsmin value the lives of all living creatures, sometimes even above our own. In contrast, men consider human life to be all important.*

"So what? Why's that such a bad thing?"

It becomes a bad thing when even the most ruthless actions are justified because they preserve the wellbeing of mankind. Have I never told you, our word for "human" means "despoiler" in your language?

James felt bewildered at her harsh words. It sounded like she'd said he was "spoiled." Only Lindsey had ever called him "spoiled." He thought it meant "pampered, babied." Surely Z'Nia wasn't calling him a baby! Could a baby have gotten her out of that cage or smuggled her onto that truck? Didn't she appreciate anything he'd done for her?

"How can you say that about me?" he asked. "You don't know what I've gone through to help you. You don't know—"

She shook her head and turned away. She didn't look back.

So that's it, he thought, his confusion morphing into anger. *After all I've done, she won't even listen to me.*

He watched her climb the hillside. Because the slope was steeper here and peppered with small jagged rocks, she could not sprint those fifty feet. For the minute or so it would take her to move across that treeless area, she'd be in full view of anyone looking her way. And now, because she was so stubborn, so unreasonable, he could do nothing to help.

But as he watched that weary figure, his anger drained away.

It was my fault she got mad, he thought. *I deserved it. I shouldn't have lied to her. I ruined everything.*

Wanting to tell her that, he sent out a silent call to her, *Z'Nia, wait!*

But she didn't look back. He knew she didn't want to hear from him right now. Maybe never again.

She had nearly reached the ridge line when James heard someone shout from below. He saw Z'Nia falter and sent her a message.

Keep going. Don't give him time to aim.

He held his breath, wishing she would go faster. Silhouetted against the sky, Z'Nia made a perfect target. He heard a loud noise, a gunshot! And then she fell to the ground.

Are you okay? he asked. *Can you get up?*

Z'Nia did not answer.

His mind-link felt like a scream. *Z'Nia, get up!*

But she did not reply. And she did not move.

CHAPTER 29

Lindsey

Even before their father turned off the ignition, Lindsey and Josh opened the car doors and got out. Dad had parked at the base of the hillside, near two other vehicles.

"The McAfees are here," Dad said. "Slade, too."

A loud *bang* resounded across the hills.

"That's a gunshot," Josh said. He started up the slope.

Dad called out, "Josh, wait!"

But Josh kept going, and the others chased after him. As she crested the hill, Lindsey saw a man standing on top of the opposite slope. Though she couldn't see his face, she thought it was Slade. He held a gun in his hand.

"What are you doing?" her mother screamed.

Mom was right, Lindsey thought. *We should have called the police.*

The Bradens ran down into the hollow to join the McAfees, who were staring at Slade. Barry's mouth formed a round O. His mother looked like she was ready to faint.

"That's our son out there!" Dad shouted.

Slade turned toward them.

"I didn't even see your kid," he said, his voice loud with anger. "I'm shooting at my animal. I own her, and I'll do what I like with her. And right now, I aim to kill her. That's if she's not dead already. I think I hit her."

Lindsey shuddered. She remembered what Matt said about Slade's poor aim. If he'd hit something, it might easily have been James.

Mom whispered, "No."

"She went down," Slade said. "I'm going over to see if I got her."

"No, you're not," Dad said.

Slade pointed the gun toward the Bradens. They froze.

Mr. McAfee pushed his wife and son behind a wall of exposed rock at the base of the slope.

"Let's just calm down," Dad said.

Behind his back, he waved his hand toward the left. Lindsey knew he wanted his family to join the McAfees behind that wall of rock. She took a half step toward it.

"You can't tell me what to do," Slade yelled.

He waved the gun. "See? This gives me a license to do whatever I want. I'm going to go see if I got her, and you can't stop me."

Lindsey slid another half step closer to the McAfees. Beside her, Josh stooped down to tie his shoelace.

And he calls me a "neat freak," she thought. *We're facing a drunken, gun-wielding crazy person, and he's worried about tripping over a shoelace!*

Josh straightened abruptly, and Lindsey saw a blur of movement. A baseball-sized rock hit Slade in the shoulder. He staggered, nearly dropping the gun.

"You shouldn't have done that," he said.

He stared at the thin stripe of blood crawling down his right sleeve. Then he grasped the gun with both hands, now extended at arm's length.

"Look out!" Dad shouted.

They all dove behind the rock wall. Even as she pressed against its rough surface, Lindsey heard another gunshot. A bullet hit the earth a few feet behind her. Dirt sprayed across the back of her legs.

Slade laughed. "That's right. Stay there. All of you."

They waited. Lindsey held her breath, listening for footsteps coming down the hillside. She imagined Slade creeping toward them to get a better aim. But she heard nothing.

Suddenly, four more shots rang out, one right after the other. None of them hit anywhere near Lindsey.

Josh muttered, "He's just trying to scare us."

"It's working," Lindsey replied softly.

She heard a series of clicks, and then everything got quiet. Her skin prickled with fear. Was he coming?

Anyone can hit something if they're close enough, she thought.

After a few moments, her father spoke. "It's okay. He emptied his revolver, and then he ran off. He's gone now."

Slowly, Lindsey raised her face and saw the others cautiously moving out into the open.

"I'm sorry," Mr. McAfee said. "Barry talked us into coming here. He said your son mentioned how much he liked this place. Slade must have decided it was worth a try."

"It's not my fault," Barry said.

His father silenced him with a look.

"That man is crazy," Mom said. "He shot at James!"

Mr. McAfee nodded. "Yes, but he's reckless, and he drinks, and now he's injured, too. He's not a good marksman. He may not have hit anything at all. If he did, it had to be purely by accident."

"Hope you're right," Dad said. "I'm going after him. I don't want him chasing James, even with an empty gun."

"I'll go with you," Josh said. "In case there's trouble."

Lindsey would have liked to go, too, but she might slow them down. Unlike Josh, she'd never done much hiking, and she didn't know these woods. Mom must have been thinking the same thing.

"I hate being left behind, but I wouldn't be much help to you," she said. "Lindsey and I will call the police."

"Yes, it's time to do that now," Dad said.

He turned to Mr. McAfee. "I know it's not likely, but Slade might come back. Will you stay until the police get here?"

"Sure," Mr. McAfee said. "We'll need to talk to them anyway about what we saw before you arrived."

So it was settled. The McAfees went back to their car, and Mrs. Braden went with them. She planned to call the police immediately.

Only Lindsey remained, watching Dad and Josh climb up to the ridge line and disappear behind the next hill.

I'm being silly, she thought. *If I've learned anything, it's that watching someone won't keep the danger away.*

She was reminded now of an autumn day much like this one, the day her younger brother disappeared. Dad and Josh had gone off in search of James, and they'd come back without him. After three horrible days, James had returned on his own. Because he never told them where he'd been, Lindsey had worried he might vanish again. In reality, there had been little danger of that happening.

That creature Matt told us about would never have come after James. Now he really is in danger from a crazy man with a gun, she thought. *All my watching and worrying didn't prevent it.*

She heard someone call out and turned to see her mother waving at her from across the hollow.

"Lindsey! That man is still out there somewhere! Come sit in the car with me."

Lindsey took one last look at the deserted hillside. Then she joined her mother, and they went back to wait for the police.

ை   ை   ை

James

James had put aside his argument with Z'Nia and hurried to help her. From close up, he could see the bright red blood trickling down her back.

Wake up, he'd said. *Slade's going to come after us. You have to wake up!*

After what had seemed like a long time, she'd finally stirred.

Help me up, she'd said.

But you're hurt.

Yes, and I will be dead if Slade discovers us. As will you. You had better come with me.

From the direction of the hollow James had heard the sound of another gunshot. Though the shot was not directed toward him and Z'Nia, he'd wondered why Slade was not yet pursuing them.

You're right, he'd told her. *Let's go.*

He'd found a stout branch Z'Nia could use as a walking stick and then helped her up.

Which way?

She'd pointed. *Northeast.*

They'd started off. Only a couple of minutes later, another series of loud bangs had echoed across the hills. Four more gunshots. They hurried on.

Now, James asked Z'Nia, *Are you sure this is the fastest way?*

It is the most direct route.

But their path took them through dense brush. They had to step over the trunks of fallen trees. Some crumbled at a touch, spilling out insects and small animals that had made their homes in the hollow logs. Others were so large that James had to lead Z'Nia around them.

Saplings grew everywhere, blocking their way. James pushed them aside and helped Z'Nia slide past, only to encounter thickets of wild blackberry bushes. The thorny canes scratched his face and hands, and the few remaining berries left sweet-smelling stains on his jacket.

The forest has grown out of control, Z'Nia said.

Because you were not here, James replied.

Yes. At least in part.

You'll get it back under control, he said.

Z'Nia did not reply, and they continued walking.

James knew the trek through the woods was sapping her strength. He had based his plan on a healthy, strong Z'Nia who could outrun most animals and climb the tallest trees. Instead, she could manage no more than a steady walk. Even that required his help.

He asked her, *How much farther?*

The distance of our journey from the circus grounds to the farmer's field. And back again.

A half mile. For him, not far at all. But for Z'Nia, it would be a long way. He knew she couldn't do it alone. If she didn't let him help her get home, she might not make it there at all.

Couldn't you trust me again? he asked. *I'm really sorry we had to leave the other animals behind.*

She didn't look at him.

All his thoughts came out in a rush. *I was afraid we'd get caught. I couldn't figure out what to do, and there wasn't time to make another plan.*

Still she did not meet his gaze.

So you lied, she said.

James heaved a sigh. *I knew we'd never be able to free them. It was hard enough freeing you.*

She gave no sign that she had heard. James felt miserable.

I did the best I could, he said, but it sounded like a weak excuse.

We cannot do only what is easy, she told him. *We must choose to do what is right.*

James didn't know how to respond. He wondered if life was really that cut-and-dried. Was everything supposed to be either right or wrong? No gray areas?

A couple of days ago, he might have agreed with that. Then, his choices were about things like obeying his parents, paying attention in school, or following the rules in gym class. Not too complicated, usually.

But so much had happened since then. Now he was on the run from some psycho who'd already shot Z'Nia and wanted to kill her. What was he supposed to do? Take care of Z'Nia, right? Oh, yeah, and try not to get shot himself. That was important, too, wasn't it?

But Z'Nia might say freeing the circus animals was just as important. She might be less worried about her own survival than about making sure no one else was harmed.

James shook his head. He didn't understand.

Maybe I can keep us both alive somehow, he thought. *I'll have to do my best.*

It still sounded weak, but it was all he had.

CHAPTER 30

James

They'd been walking for another ten minutes when James first noticed the sound. *Thrash*. It came from somewhere behind them.

The hairs rose on the back of his neck.

What is that? he asked Z'Nia.

Z'Nia didn't answer. She plodded beside him, all her attention on the simple task of placing one foot in front of the other.

He tugged at her arm.

That sound. Is it Slade?

Her step faltered. She gazed into the distance, concentrating. Soon she started walking again.

Slade is following us, she said.

I was afraid of that, James replied.

She drew in a labored breath. *But the sound you hear is made by an animal.*

He asked her what kind of animal made that much noise.

Bear, she told him, and she continued walking in her slow, steady pace.

James felt his heartbeat quicken. He knew black bears lived in this part of the country. So late in October, he would expect most of them to be hibernating.

Maybe we disturbed it, he thought, recalling a large, hollow log they'd scrambled across.

He knew black bears rarely attacked humans, and that made him feel a little better.

Then he realized, *Z'Nia's not human. And she's wounded besides. Could the bear have smelled the blood? Could it know she's weak?*

When he asked her about that, she said, *Probably.*

James didn't like that answer.

Maybe it's not a bear, he told her. *It could be a deer, couldn't it? Or even a good-sized raccoon?*

Z'Nia's gaze met his.

It is a bear, James, she said.

He heard the thrashing noise again. Was it closer now? He turned his head to the left, then to the right, trying to figure out where that bear might be. He couldn't tell for sure.

He knew Z'Nia would be unable to resist an attack. He'd have to defend her. Again, he wished he knew more about fighting, though he didn't think wrestling lessons would be much use against a bear.

James reached into his pocket for his Swiss Army knife. It wasn't much of a weapon, but it was all he had. Except he didn't have it after all. He must have lost it when he'd rolled under the truck.

He looked around, desperate to find some kind of weapon, but he couldn't see anything useful. Then Z'Nia's words came back to him, that humans always put their own needs first.

But I'm not, he thought. *It's her I'm trying to protect.*

And a little voice inside his head asked, *Are you sure she'd want you to do that?*

Confused, James gave up looking for a weapon. He didn't know if he could take on a bear anyway.

He said, *We'll have to stay ahead of the bear. And Slade, too.*

They moved on. But now James imagined every shadow hid some danger and every sound signaled a threat closing in on them.

They passed the crumbling shell of a cabin. The stone foundation and some rotting logs were all that showed where a pioneer family must have lived.

And died, James thought as he spied a tiny graveyard.

Just looking at it made him shiver. Its three lonely headstones leaned in various directions, as if no one had cared about this place for a long, long time. Only a few birds nesting in the remains of the old chimney lived here now.

But although the woods felt deserted, James knew he and Z'Nia were not alone. Somewhere behind them, a bear continued stalking its prey. Somewhere, Slade was doing the same. He wished they could move just a little faster.

Finally, he pushed through a bramble bush and held the branches aside so Z'Nia could pass. When he turned to move forward again, he saw they had entered a small clearing. To their left, the woods thinned out dramatically.

Z'Nia pointed in that direction. *The river is just beyond those trees.*

About time, James thought.

She stumbled toward a large rock and leaned against it.

I must rest for a few minutes, she said. *Will you see what lies ahead?*

He listened for that thrashing sound but heard nothing. Other than a trio of crows in a nearby tree, he could see no animals at all. Could the bear have given up? Might it have found an easier target? He wanted to believe that.

Okay, he said.

James soon found the river. He estimated the Cambria's width at about a hundred feet, not that wide as rivers go. Steep banks sloped down to muddy water that appeared to be only moderately deep. He thought a good swimmer could manage the swift current, but he doubted if Z'Nia would be able to handle it. Not today. Even her mind-link sounded weak now.

Not sure I could do it, either, he admitted. After a nearly sleepless night and a cross-country hike, he felt bone weary. He'd just have to make sure neither of them fell into the water.

He bent over, hands on knees, trying to catch his breath. He allowed himself only a few seconds of rest and then straightened to return to Z'Nia.

As he did so, he became aware of a strange sensation. Ever since last night, Z'Nia's presence had been in his head. Whenever they used the mind-link to communicate, James felt that presence strongly. But even when she refused to speak to him, he'd been conscious of her in a more passive way, as if they had some permanent connection. Now, without warning, the connection was fading.

He thought about what that might mean and raced back to the clearing, afraid he'd find her lying unconscious on the ground. But she was exactly where he'd left her, leaning against the same rock. Only now she was staring at Slade. The man stood opposite Z'Nia, pointing his gun at her.

"Leave her alone!" James shouted.

He ran over and got between them.

Why did you come back? Z'Nia asked.

James could hear the sorrow in her tone. He knew she'd tried to protect him by sending him away and cutting off their mental connection.

"I know you," Slade said. "You're the boy who wanted to see bigfoot."

James turned to face him. His gaze fastened on the gun, which was now pointed in his direction.

Slade laughed. "I'm here to get my property. Dead or alive, you might say, but right now, I'm thinking dead is better."

"She's never done a thing to you," James said. "Leave her alone, or I'll report you to ..."

He wasn't sure who to call about threats to a species most people had never heard of.

"... to the Humane Society."

It felt like a lame thing to say, but he could think of nothing better.

"Sure, kid. You go ahead. Call the governor. Call the White House for all I care. Who'd listen to you anyway? It's your word against mine."

James clenched his fists, but he knew it was a useless gesture. Slade was a couple of inches taller than he was. More muscular, too. Oh, yeah. And he still had that gun.

His mind raced. *This man is crazy enough to shoot Z'Nia. Maybe even me. What can I do?*

Just a few days ago, when he'd decided that freeing Z'Nia was worth a fight, he'd never expected to be facing an armed man. Especially not by himself. But he and Z'Nia were on their own. Help would not be coming.

"Are you going to move?" Slade asked.

Jaw set, James shook his head.

"Come on, boy. I just reloaded this thing. There's enough bullets in here for both of you, but it's bigfoot I'm after. You just get out of the way."

Behind him, James heard movement.

He's bluffing. You stay back! he told Z'Nia.

I will do what must be done, she replied.

A moment later, the gun barrel shifted to the right. James saw Z'Nia standing unsteadily beside him. He started to move in front of her again, but Slade stopped him.

"You move and I'll shoot her," he said.

James froze, his thoughts spinning. *I don't know what to do. If I try to protect her, Slade will shoot. And if I just stand here, he'll shoot anyway.*

He remembered what Z'Nia had said about the defensive instincts she tried to restrain. Was she feeling them now? Wouldn't this be the time for her to defend herself? But, no, she didn't want to hurt anyone. Maybe not even a bad guy like Slade.

It's up to me, James realized. *What should I do?*

Slade smiled at him unpleasantly. "She's about three-fourths dead anyway. One bullet should be enough. And after I'm done with her, you and I will have a little talk."

"We don't have anything to talk about," James said.

Slade's voice hardened. "Oh, I think we do. Like how you snooped through my belongings. You're going to tell me everything you know about that."

He's seen that overturned carton, James thought. His heartbeat skipped wildly.

Slade looked back at Z'Nia. He raised the gun and aimed it at her forehead.

James made his decision. He would try to grab the gun. He knew Slade's aim was lousy. Even this close to his target, there was a chance he'd miss.

I'm counting on that, James thought.

He bent his knees, ready to lunge forward, but Slade's eyes widened. The man stumbled away from Z'Nia, nearly dropping his gun.

What's going on? James wondered. *He's acting like he did when he saw the spider. Only worse.*

Then he glanced toward Z'Nia, and he understood. Just a dozen feet behind her loomed a large black bear. It had tracked them through the forest, and now it had found them.

CHAPTER 31

James

James had never seen a bear outside the zoo. At nearly six feet tall, this one seemed huge. Except for its brown snout, it was entirely black. Black coat. Black eyes. Curved black claws, wickedly sharp. It smelled of damp leaves and grass.

The bear looked at Z'Nia. She did not flinch.

Move, James told her. *Can't you see, it's sizing you up for dinner?*

But she stood firm.

Trying to protect me again, he thought.

James tried to push her out of the bear's path, but she refused to budge. The bear snorted loudly.

A shot rang out, and James ducked instinctively. Relieved to find himself unharmed, he looked at Z'Nia. She also seemed to have escaped further injury.

The bear roared, whether in pain or outrage James could not tell. It lumbered past him, its gaze now fixed on Slade. One massive paw swiped at the man's shoulder. As Slade fell, his gun flew off in a wide arc. His sleeve hung in shreds, and a long scratch on his upper arm oozed blood.

Slade scrambled across the ground, his head jerking from side to side.

He's looking for that gun, I'll bet, James thought. *No way I'm letting him have it.*

Half-a-second later, he and Slade both spotted it lying at the base of a nearby tree. Slade lunged for it, but James got there first. He kicked it hard. It skidded across the clearing and came to rest in a pile of leaves.

Slade started to crawl after it. But with a bellow that terrified James to his toes, the bear moved in. Now Slade couldn't get the gun without passing the bear. It turned and confronted him.

Slade tried to speak, but James couldn't understand him. Was he calling for help?

James searched his memory for information about bears.

"Back away slowly," he said, trying to keep his voice steady. "You

143

can't outrun a bear. And don't look it in the eye. It might think you're challenging it."

But Slade's terror wouldn't let him listen. He staggered to his feet. Then, his eyes wild with panic, he ran off into the trees. The growling bear followed.

James stared after it. He turned back to speak to Z'Nia, but the words caught in his throat. On the branches above her head, dozens of crows now perched like silent, black-winged sentinels. Their shiny eyes focused on the path the bear had taken. With a chorus of harsh cries, they flew off in pursuit.

When the sound of their flapping wings had died away, a single bird remained. It was a tiny sparrow. As it flew to Z'Nia's shoulder, James saw its left wing was slightly imperfect. The bird chirped a few notes, sweet and shrill, that brought a smile to her face. Then it flew off.

James smiled, too, amazed to be seeing that sparrow at last.

You did take care of it, he said. *I hoped you would.*

Of course. That little bird continued to visit me from time to time. I am glad she has survived in my absence.

Me, too, James said. Then, reluctantly, he added, *I guess we should do something to help Slade.*

He wondered if Z'Nia could tell that he'd rather not.

Do not worry, she replied. *If the bear wanted to catch him, it would already have done so. It is simply chasing him away from us.*

She leaned back against her rock. Pain had etched deep creases across her forehead and beside her mouth.

I did not intend for that to happen, she said.

James asked, *What do you mean?*

The crows must have summoned the bear to help us. But I would not have called it. I would not have put its life in danger.

Not even to save our lives? James asked.

She smiled wearily. *To save yours, perhaps. I admit I was tempted. I wonder what my mother would think about that.*

Wouldn't she want you to save yourself?

Z'Nia shook her head. *Mother always stressed that I should choose to do only what is right. She said that would shape my identity as a Tazsmin. But I realize now that I am more than a member of a dying species. I am Z'Nia, too. And as Z'Nia, I see that right and wrong may not be so clearly defined. Perhaps, after all, I can only do my best.*

Though she would say no more about it, James thought she had forgiven him. As if to confirm that, she asked him to help her walk to the river. They went very slowly. Twice she stopped to rest, and once she paused to look at the shredded bark on a tree.

A deer caused this damage, she said. *But I do not have the strength to heal it.*

You can come back when you're feeling better, James told her.

Z'Nia ran her fingers over the scarred tree trunk. *Do you really believe that?*

James looked at her. She seemed so weak. Did he believe she'd recover? He wasn't sure. Humans were accustomed to saying positive things when people were ill, but Z'Nia would not welcome a lie.

He said only, *We should go on.*

At last, they reached the curve where the river angled east. James felt her excitement.

We made it, he thought.

But when they turned the corner, James saw what awaited them. Neither his own sparse memories nor Z'Nia's descriptions had prepared him for this. The water flowed over a rock formation towering far above his head, then plunged into a basin below. The pool beneath the falls churned furiously and sent up little plumes of mist.

Too much rain, Z'Nia said.

James saw many little streams draining down the steep banks to swell the river. He knew there would be more such streams above the falls.

Z'Nia stared at her waterfall.

I cannot get to my cave without your help, she said.

That's okay, James replied. *I wanted to help you anyway.*

She showed him where to find the steps her mother had chiseled into the canyon wall.

I don't see them, he said.

Z'Nia pointed. *There, under the vines.*

James looked again. He saw how vines and moss had covered the steps in her absence. Getting down to the cave would not be easy.

We'll do it together, James said.

He went first. Z'Nia told him just where to place his feet, just how to lean in to the wall to maintain his balance. The wind pushed at them, and he steadied her. They inched along, sharing the danger.

James tried to keep his mind on the moment. He didn't want to think about what Z'Nia would do once they reached the cave. He didn't want to believe she could be going home to die.

The stairs took them to a narrow ledge. Just below, the Cambria lapped hungrily at their feet. They slid sideways for a few careful steps, and then the ledge ended.

There is one last step, Z'Nia said. She pointed out a boulder that protruded through the spray.

Yes. I see it. Up a little and to the left.

It was almost five feet from where he now stood. Getting onto that boulder would require a big step for her, a leap for him. He suggested she go first in case she needed help. But Z'Nia pointed out that James stood between her and the cave, and there was little room for maneuvering on this ledge. Besides, though she could hardly stand on her own, she claimed the right to see him safely through the falls before she followed him.

You're stubborn, he said. *And proud.*

She didn't reply.

James couldn't tell whether she agreed with him or simply lacked the energy to argue. Either way, he knew she wouldn't give in, so he got ready to jump.

Expecting the waterfall to push him downward, he flexed his knees to get as much power behind his leap as he could. Then he launched himself across space, through the falling water, and into the cave. He rolled forward on impact and landed in a heap against the wall. When he looked up, he saw an image of himself as a three-year-old. He knew Z'Nia had painted it.

He turned toward the entrance and waited. Though his clothes were soaked, and the cave was cold, it was Z'Nia that worried him. He wished he could step outside and extend his hand to her. But the lip of the boulder wasn't large enough for both of them to stand there at the same time.

He could see little beyond that wall of water. Still, he stood beside it, ready to help her the moment she appeared. He waited … and waited.

James remembered the depth of the river and the speed of the current. If Z'Nia had fallen into the water, she'd be in danger of drowning.

He decided to go back through the falls just to make sure she was okay. And then that icy curtain parted, and Z'Nia crashed onto the floor of the cave.

I thought you'd never get here, James said.

But she didn't answer. She didn't even move.

He knelt on the floor next to her and rolled her onto her side. Her wound, he saw, had stopped oozing blood, but he wasn't sure what that meant. Her face looked gray. She didn't appear to be breathing. James held one hand near her parted lips, trying to detect even the slightest breath. He felt nothing.

The jump was too much, he thought. *It's killed her.*

He sat back on his heels. *How could this happen after all we've been through? I can't just leave her like this.*

He didn't know what to do. Hoping his subconscious would send him an idea, he stared at the waterfall and tried to lose his thoughts in its vast flow. It didn't work.

"No one even knows where I am," he murmured. "There's no one to help me."

Then, without warning, Z'Nia gasped. It was a shallow breath, but a breath all the same. She opened her eyes.

James, she said.

Just that one word. And then she closed her eyes again.

CHAPTER 32

James

"Z'Nia," James said. "Please be okay."

Her eyes fluttered open, then closed once more. She seemed unaware of his presence.

Frantic to do something to help her, he mentally reviewed the basic first-aid he'd learned in the Cub Scouts. He remembered how to stop a nose bleed, handle an insect bite, or care for minor cuts and scrapes. He knew nothing about gunshot wounds.

"She's unconscious," he muttered. "Mr. Jessup didn't cover that. Do I raise her head? Tip it back? I don't know what to do."

He wished he could just call 911.

I'll make her comfortable, he decided. That seemed like a safe choice.

Using wood she had gathered years before, he built a small fire below the smoke hole. He covered her with blankets she had woven from plant fibers. Though he could find no food in the cave, he filled a gourd with water from the falls. But when he held it to her lips, she could not drink.

She lay motionless for so long that he feared she had died. Only the slight movement of her eyes beneath their lids told him she was still alive.

James sat beside her to keep watch. As he stared into the fire, images from the past flashed through his mind. He began telling Z'Nia about them.

"I remember this place," he said. "You showed me your paintings and your arrowheads. I remember how the waterfall sounded like thunder."

He went on talking, his voice a soft drone in the otherwise silent cave. He spoke of the lessons she had taught him and told her how often he'd looked for her over the years. And he let her know how glad he was that he'd found her again.

"I'll always remember you," he told her.

James continued watching for any sign that Z'Nia would regain consciousness. When he'd nearly given up hope, she opened her eyes at last.

I must prepare myself, she said.

On the journey to Richland, she had described the Tazsmin burial traditions in some detail. He knew her mother's body lay on a stone shelf deep within the cave and that Z'Nia had created a similar resting place for herself. She wanted to go there now, to lie near her mother. But she hadn't the energy to walk that far, and he lacked the strength to carry her.

Stay here by the fire, he suggested at last. *You can look up and see your paintings.*

Z'Nia managed a weak nod.

Then he opened his pack and removed two of his most precious possessions, a perfect pinecone and an arrowhead worn smooth by time. Just as she had once put them in his hands, he now placed them in hers.

She smiled and curled her fingers around them.

Will you say the prayers now? she asked.

Despite his earlier promises to help Z'Nia with her death rites, James could not bring himself to do it.

"Not yet," he said aloud.

It is time. You know what to do.

His throat ached as if a chestnut had lodged there. "No, it's too soon."

You said you would help, she reminded him. Her mind-link was growing faint.

James couldn't refuse.

He searched his thoughts for the phrases she had recited that morning. Instead, his mind showed him Z'Nia bending to heal the leaf of a fern. And the only words that came to him were those of the WindSinger as she repaired the broken wing of a dying sparrow.

"I've forgotten the words for your ritual," he said.

She did not respond.

So he tried a mental message. *Help me remember what I need to say.*

But she gave no sign that she could hear him.

Is it too late? he wondered. *No, it can't be. I promised to help her, and I won't let her down. I'll just have to do what I can.*

He rested one hand on her shoulder, hoping she would know he was still with her.

"You're not alone," he said aloud.

149

Then he recited the part of the ritual he still remembered.

"Grow in love. Grow in peace."

Those familiar healing words were also the very last lines of her death prayer.

Smoke rose from the fire as his chant filled the once-silent cave. As if to bid her good-by, the sound of the wind came, too. It whispered her name, and with every word he spoke, the volume grew. Soon, James could hear nothing else. Not his own voice. Not even the roar of the falls.

He continued to say those Tazsmin words, the only ones he knew. He repeated them until the flames had faded to a heap of glowing embers. And he sat beside Z'Nia as the embers died and the sound of the wind finally blew away.

When it was all over, James felt drained. He leaned back and rested his head against the wall of the cave, too tired to think, almost too tired to feel.

It's done, he thought. *I did all I could. I hope it was good enough.*

He didn't move for what seemed like a long time. Then he suddenly remembered the world outside. The slippery steps beside the waterfall made for a dangerous climb. If he didn't leave soon, the rising water would make it impossible. With a deep sigh, he reached for one of Z'Nia's blankets and used it to cover her face. He'd seen people do that on TV shows. It felt like the respectful thing to do.

"Good-bye," he whispered.

He hated to leave, but he had no choice. It was already after one o'clock. His family had probably reached the hollow by now. Once they saw he wasn't there, they'd come looking for him. If he wanted Z'Nia to remain undisturbed, he had to avoid drawing attention to the waterfall. He wanted to be well away from it by the time anyone found him.

Dragging himself to his feet, James thought about the climb back up the ravine. The hardest part would be getting onto that narrow ledge. When he'd jumped from the ledge into the cave, his momentum had carried him into a forward roll. But leaping back the other way would require him to make a firm landing.

That ledge is too narrow for me to roll forward or even move very much, he thought. *The jump will be a lot harder this time.*

He went to the cave's entrance. Though water splashed down all around him, a ledge above his head protected him from some of the downpour. He got ready to make the leap but stopped himself at the last minute.

Something looked different. Through the spray, he saw a series of hand- and foot-holds cut into the rock wall beside the falls. He knew he hadn't seen them before he'd entered the cave. That part of the wall had been covered by vines. Now, most of them had been ripped away.

He remembered how Z'Nia had urged him ahead of her, down the rough steps and behind the falls. And he remembered how long he'd had to wait before she finally entered the cave. He realized she had spent precious minutes clearing the vines that had grown in her absence. She'd wanted to help him scale that wall.

Her voice seemed to echo through his mind: *We Tazsmin value the lives of all living creatures, sometimes even above our own.*

She valued my life above hers, he thought.

He felt bad about it. He made himself a promise, that he'd get home safely so her sacrifice wouldn't be wasted.

Deciding his backpack would just get in the way, James tossed it aside. Except for a couple of empty water bottles, there wasn't much in it anyway.

Then he stood on the boulder at the mouth of the cave. He leaned out to grip the nearest hand-hold with his left hand and set his left foot directly below it. He could see where he'd have to position his right hand and foot. But that would require him to leave the safety of the boulder, with the river rushing just below him.

"Now or never," he muttered.

He swung himself onto that rocky wall and scrambled to get his right hand and foot into place. Passing through the waterfall had drenched him again. Carefully, he leaned his head sideways and wiped his face against the dry underside of his sleeve. Now, at least he could see.

The sound of the falls seemed overwhelming. Then, from somewhere above, the cry of a solitary bird cut through the water's roar. James wanted to believe this was one of the crows who had chased after Slade and the bear. Maybe it wanted to help him.

There's nothing it can do for me, he thought. But still, he felt grateful for its presence.

He pressed his body against the rock. If he wanted to maintain his balance, he couldn't lean back or move his head very much. He'd have to find the next hand- and foot-holds by touch alone. James forced himself to slide his right hand across the wall, but his fingers found only a solid surface. He felt the first flickers of panic.

Where is it? he wondered. *Where's the next hold?*

It occurred to him that the holds were spaced to be comfortable for a Tazsmin, not a human boy. He stretched higher but succeeded only in scraping his wrist on a sharp edge of the rock.

If I can't find it, I'll have to go back to the cave, he thought. He could think of no other choice.

And then his hand touched an inch-wide crack. He jammed his fingers into it.

James took a few deep breaths to quiet his racing heart before trying to move again. This time, he found a place to set his right foot almost immediately. Though small, that jutting bit of stone did support his weight. But the new holds left him spreadeagled across the face of the rock. It didn't feel safe. He started to shift his left hand and foot into more comfortable positions.

As he did so, he spied some movement out of the corner of his eye. He heard a kind of fluttering sound, and something brushed against his hair. Could it be the bird, maybe wanting to encourage him?

He looked up, trying to see, but he moved too quickly. His left foot missed its hold. At the same time, his right foot started to slip. He struggled to get it back into place, but he couldn't do it. Without warning, he found himself suspended from the rock face, his hands supporting all his weight.

James barely had time to understand his predicament when his fingers started to slip, too.

No! he thought. He knew the ledge was only a few feet to his right. He tried to swing his body in that direction, but there wasn't enough time.

He lost hold and slid down the rock, his fingers scraping uselessly against it. As he plunged into the water, he glimpsed a black-feathered bird clinging to a remnant of vine on the rock face. Then, before he could take even one breath, he sank beneath the surface.

CHAPTER 33

James

Stunned by the cold water, James almost forgot to move his arms and legs. He couldn't escape the noise of the water. It seemed to surround him.

A voice inside his head told him to swim. He struggled to move from under the waterfall, but the current tumbled him, scrambling his sense of direction. Confused, he stopped fighting and drifted aimlessly. And then he felt rock beneath his feet.

It must be the bottom of the basin, he thought.

He kicked hard, fighting to get to the surface. Instead, the current thrust him sideways and slammed him headfirst against a rock. His neck bent sharply to one side. Pain flared in his left shoulder. It shot down his arm and into his hand. His arm instantly went slack.

Dazed, James wondered, *What just happened? Did I break my arm?*

He had never experienced anything like this. Disoriented, he floated away from the boulder. Though his arm remained limp, the pain quickly receded to a tingling sensation. He hoped that meant his injury wasn't serious, but he had little time to think about it.

By now, his lungs were on fire. His head pounded and his throat ached from holding his breath. Light pulsed across the inside of his eyelids. He knew he had to breathe soon, but he couldn't focus on how to make that happen. The noise and the cold seemed to have muddled his thoughts.

Then the current moved him again, and he was no longer directly under the waterfall. James hugged his left arm across his body, ready to swim with the other. He pushed against the riverbed once more, careful to steer clear of boulders. A moment later, his head burst above the surface.

He turned his face upwards and sucked in great gulps of air. Thankful just to breath again, he floated on his back. He thought he would rest for a few minutes, and then he'd figure out what to do next.

But within seconds, the river began carrying him downstream. He saw leaves and sticks bobbing on the surface and tried to shove them out of his way. A large branch grazed his head as it drifted by. Then a submerged pine tree snagged his feet, and he had to kick free before it pulled him under.

Everything's happening too fast, he thought. For the first time, he felt afraid.

James tried to concentrate, but his brain still seemed sluggish. Some important fact lay at the back of his mind, nagging insistently. What was it? He knew cold water would lower his body temperature. Already, he was shivering violently. Could his brain be affected as well? Would that keep him from thinking clearly?

His fear grew.

James forgot to watch for floating debris. He crashed into a small tree that had fallen into the river. The impact sent a jolt of pain through his injured shoulder. He grabbed at the tree with his right hand, but his fingers felt thick, clumsy. They slid off the tree trunk and the current swept him away. The Cambria angled left, and James went with it.

Pay attention, he ordered himself.

He ignored the fear and started preparing for the next chance to grab a fallen tree. But he was conscious again that he'd forgotten something important. An image of the map he'd shown Z'Nia entered his mind. He pictured the direction the river had taken.

This part of the river flows right around Richland, he remembered. *If I don't get out of the water soon, the current will carry me miles beyond the hollow.*

James looked up at the riverbanks rising on either side of him. They didn't look as steep or as high as the walls flanking the waterfall. Trees and bushes had sprouted on their sloping sides. If he could grab one, he could use it to pull himself out of the water. He began looking for a tree growing near the waterline.

But something still nagged at him. He knew there was a flaw in his plan. He just couldn't see what it was.

He visualized himself reaching out with his right hand, grasping a tree, pulling himself onto the land and climbing upwards. But when he tried to imagine what would happen next, he knew he'd made a mistake.

That's it! That's what I've been trying to remember, he thought. *The hollow is on my left, but I've been angling toward the right bank. If I get out on that side of the river, there are no bridges I can cross to get back.*

154

Stroking awkwardly, James changed direction and began swimming toward the opposite bank. He had to go across the current. If he'd been less tired and had the use of both arms, he could have managed that distance in a couple of minutes. But his injury slowed him down. The strength of the current seemed to cancel out two of every three strokes he took.

Finally, as he approached the left bank, he saw a fallen branch protruding into the water.

I'm going too fast, he thought. *I'll miss it.*

Summoning all his energy, he hurled his body toward the branch. His fingers brushed against it, skidded along its surface, then came away empty. The river carried him onward.

Determined, James gritted his teeth and got ready to try again. Spying a bush growing just above the waterline, he lunged for it and managed to grab hold with his right hand. He entwined his fingers among its branches and pulled himself toward it. But rainfall had loosened the roots, and the bush came out of the earth. James fell backward, captured once more by the current.

In an instant, the water closed over his head. He kicked furiously and bobbed back to the surface, swallowing a mouthful of muddy water. He coughed it up.

I'm so tired, he thought. *So cold.*

He wanted nothing more than to lie back, close his eyes, and forget about everything. But he couldn't do that. He couldn't just give up.

Come on, this has to work, he told himself.

And it had to work soon. Within minutes, the current would carry him far downriver. He'd have a long journey back to the hollow.

If I manage to survive at all, he thought grimly. But, no, he wouldn't let himself consider that possibility.

He got back into position and tried again. This time, he had better luck. His fingers snagged a small evergreen whose roots were solidly planted. The river tugged at him, trying to wrench him loose, but he refused to let go. It seemed to take all his strength, but he finally hauled his body onto the land.

He lay there panting, too tired to move any farther. But just a few feet away, the Cambria rushed by, ready to swallow him up if he waited too long. He raised his head to view the slope he'd have to climb and breathed a sigh of relief. Though steep and slippery from the rain, this part of the bank was covered with saplings he could use to pull himself up.

He pushed himself onto his knees and unconsciously reached out with his left arm.

It's better, he realized. *I can move it.*

Even the tingling had subsided. With two usable arms, it took him only a few minutes to reach the top of the ravine. He levered his body over its upper edge.

I made it, he thought. *And in one piece, more or less.*

Though his shoulder still felt tender, he could move it freely. His head throbbed from hitting that underwater rock, and he had some painful scrapes on his hands. But other than that, he could detect no serious injuries. He thought he'd been lucky.

Now all he had to do was find his way out of the forest. He staggered to his feet, faced away from the water and looked around to get his bearings.

I know this place, he thought.

Miraculously, he'd come out of the river at almost the exact spot where he'd first seen it. Directly ahead of him was the tree Z'Nia had been unable to heal. James stumbled over to it and laid one hand across its damaged bark just as she had done. Her song seemed to echo through his mind.

"Grow in love. Grow in peace," he whispered. He imagined he could feel the warmth of her hand, the beat of her pulse.

She's gone, he thought. *Now there's no one to care for this tree.*

His hand fell back to his side. He turned away, no longer wanting to see the damage Z'Nia would never return to heal. A wave of fatigue spilled over him. Even turning his wrist to see the face of his watch felt like a huge task. He was relieved to see it still worked.

One thirty-five, he thought in disbelief. *I was in the water for only a few minutes. How can that be?*

It had seemed much longer. Still, he knew his family would be looking for him by now. He pressed a button on his watch to access the compass feature. Then, weary to his bones, he started off to find the hollow.

CHAPTER 34

James

James trudged through the forest, barely aware of branches arching above him, their last leaves sheltering him from the weather. Pine needles deadened the sound of his footsteps, as if he'd been sealed in a protective cocoon.

Now that he stood on dry land, a sort of delayed-action fear swept over him. He might have been killed today, not once but several times. Though he felt relieved, he could hardly stop himself from shaking.

A tangle of emotions pulled at him. He felt guilty for worrying his parents, yet unsure about what he could tell them. He grieved for Z'Nia but was grateful he'd been able to help her. And he felt angry at Slade, though he also blamed himself for what had happened. James thought those feelings might be with him for a long, long time. It would be hard to sort them all out.

A shout got his attention. "James! Over here!"

As if someone had broken open his cocoon, James suddenly noticed everything around him. He spotted birds darting among the trees. He smelled the piney scent of evergreens. And from somewhere nearby, he heard the crunch of brittle leaves being ground underfoot. When he turned toward the sound, he saw Josh hurrying in his direction.

James waited for Josh to reach him.

"Hey, little brother. You okay?"

James nodded.

Josh frowned at him. "What happened? Did you fall in the river?"

James had forgotten about his appearance. He looked down at his clothes, still damp and filthy from the muddy water.

"Yeah, I kind of did," he said.

Without another word, Josh pulled off his own jacket and draped it across his brother's shoulders.

"Come on," he said. "Everybody's waiting for us."

As they walked, Josh told him how the family had found Slade in the hollow with the McAfees.

Again, James felt guilty. "Sorry. He was mad at me. I never thought he'd shoot at anyone else."

"That guy's crazy," Josh said. "I think he just likes shooting. It makes him feel powerful."

He described how he and Dad had come across Slade again when they were searching for James in the forest. But by this time, he'd lost his gun and had appeared to be running away from something.

"He acted like he was scared out of his mind, but he didn't make much sense," Josh said. "We couldn't understand what he was running from."

James knew. "A bear."

"Really?" Josh's tone was sharp. His eyes searched the woods on both sides of them. Then he glanced back over his shoulder.

"I haven't seen any sign of a bear," Josh said. "But let's stay alert, just in case."

Certain the bear would not return, James said only, "Okay."

"No wonder Slade was so happy to see us," Josh continued. "Dad took him back to talk to the police, and I said I'd keep looking for you. That was about half an hour ago."

James nodded. He didn't feel like talking now. Josh took the hint, and they walked the rest of the way in silence.

At last they looked down into the hollow. It seemed crowded with people. The grass had been trampled flat, and even the wildflowers looked faded.

It doesn't feel right, James thought. He missed that mysterious quality he'd noticed earlier.

He saw his parents and Lindsey standing together. They weren't talking much. He figured they were worrying about him, and that made him feel guilty again.

Mr. and Mrs. McAfee stood a little to one side, watching Barry. He'd found a handful of pebbles and was lobbing them, one by one, at the boulders ringing the crest of the hill.

On the far side of the hollow, a police officer guarded Chet Slade, while his partner talked on a mobile phone. Slade sat on the ground, his head jerking from side to side.

Wonder if he's looking for a way to escape, James thought. He hoped the police would keep a close watch on the man.

Then he sighed. Everyone would have questions, questions he

couldn't or wouldn't answer. He wished he could retreat into the woods until only his family remained.

Josh seemed to understand his concerns. "We all promised to keep your secret. And you don't have to answer to Slade or the McAfees."

"But I'll have to talk to the police, won't I?" James asked.

"Yeah, you will."

"Slade's gonna say Z'Nia was his property. He's gonna say I stole her."

"He might."

James drew a deep breath. He would have to choose his words carefully. He'd have to keep Matt out of this.

"Thanks for the warning," he said.

Barry spotted them as they walked down the hill.

"Hey, there's James," he shouted. He started toward them.

Barry's father caught him by the arm and spoke to him. Barry stayed next to his dad, his face downcast.

"Sorry," he mumbled as James walked by.

"Yeah, it's okay," James replied, though it wasn't okay at all.

He suspected Barry wouldn't stay sorry for long. Once his dad no longer stood over him, he'd probably start talking to anyone who'd listen. He'd tell them how he "personally" faced a dangerous gunman and watched James make off with "the only bigfoot in captivity."

And then there'd be questions from the other kids, too. Maybe even from the teachers.

I'll have to avoid answering. I did it before, James thought.

But he'd been a little kid then. Everybody had assumed he couldn't remember what had happened. He wouldn't get by so easily this time.

He knew his family had questions of their own. To his surprise, no one pressured him for answers.

Lindsey won't be able to stop herself, he thought.

But she only smiled and held out a granola bar she'd brought from home.

"Sorry. It's a little bit crushed," she said.

James stared, astonished that his sister would offer him something she and her friend Regina called "junk food." He noticed her ruined nail polish and the loose strands of hair falling around her face. This was not the overly-careful Lindsey he knew. He took the granola bar from her hand.

"Thanks," he said.

Before he could open it, his mother wrapped him in a fierce hug. For once, James didn't mind the public display.

"Don't ever go off like that again," she said.

"I won't, Mom. I'm sorry."

Dad gently pulled him away before she could get weepy. "We'll talk later, James. Right now, the police need some information. Are you ready for that?"

James wasn't sure how to answer. He felt uneasy about talking to a police officer. But Josh came up with a blanket he'd fetched from the car, giving him a moment to think. As he returned his brother's jacket, James wondered what Slade had said. Had the man accused him of theft? He felt beads of sweat dotting his forehead as he thought about that.

"Am I in trouble?" he asked.

"I hope not," Dad said. "Whatever happens, we're on your side. Just tell the truth."

I'll tell as much of it as I can, James thought.

He'd already made up his mind to keep Z'Nia's secrets no matter what happened. And there was no way he'd let Matt share any of the blame.

As one of the officers approached, his parents moved to stand on either side of him. Josh and Lindsey stood nearby. James was glad they were all there, but he knew they couldn't help him much.

Officer Ryan introduced himself and said, "My partner will keep an eye on Mr. Slade while we talk."

"Can we do this quickly?" Mrs. Braden asked. "We have to get James home. He needs medical attention."

"Yes, Ma'am, I'll do the best I can," Officer Ryan said. He took a notebook from his pocket and looked at James. "Can you tell me what happened?"

James nodded.

"Slade was gonna kill her," he said. "I heard him say he wanted to sell her pelt."

Officer Ryan wrote that down. "Go on."

"Well," James continued, "I've always been good with animals. I found her in the woods and got her to come with me. Slade had said she was captured somewhere around here, so I thought maybe her home was nearby. I sneaked her onto a circus truck, and we hitched a ride."

James described what Slade had hidden on the truck. Officer Ryan seemed very interested in that overturned cardboard box.

"We'll check that out," he said. He jotted something in his notebook. "So what happened to the creature?"

James looked the officer straight in the eye, knowing his answer would be mostly true.

"Slade found us in the forest and said he was gonna shoot her. I thought he wanted to shoot me, too, because I knew about the stolen credit cards. But a bear scared him away just in time. After Slade ran off, we walked some more. She got weaker and weaker. Then she fell and couldn't get up again, and I couldn't move her. So I sat with her until– Well, until she stopped breathing."

The next part was important. He knew he'd have to tell a lie to protect Z'Nia's secret.

"Coming back here, I got lost and fell in the river," he said, holding up his scraped hands as evidence of the fall. "I doubt if I could find her again."

Officer Ryan noted James's injured hands and his wet clothes. Nodding, he wrote down everything James had said. Then he went off to make another call.

James blew out a long breath.

"You need to eat," his mother said, reminding him of the granola bar he still held in his hand.

He tore open the package, but he didn't take a bite. Though he knew he should be hungry, he felt like a million butterflies were swarming around in his stomach.

"You did fine," Dad said. He squeezed James's shoulder.

James had a question. "Dad?"

"What?" his father asked.

"Why did Slade act like that? Why couldn't he just let her go?"

Dad rubbed the back of his neck. "It's hard to understand why people do things. Greed, probably, or maybe just pure meanness. We may never know."

James nodded and let his gaze slide away. People could be complicated. He would never understand why Slade had behaved so cruelly.

Just like Mom and Dad will never understand why I didn't tell them about Z'Nia, he thought. Guilt gnawed at him again.

"Hey," his dad said.

James looked at him.

"You did the right thing. We're proud of you."

James managed a smile. He felt his emotions begin to untangle, just a little.

A few minutes later, Officer Ryan returned to say that James was free to go.

"Buddy Campbell confirms your boy's story," he said to Mr. and Mrs. Braden. "James didn't unlock that cage. One of the circus crew was just careless and let the animal escape. Your son simply tried to keep Slade from killing her. And Slade can't complain about his loss of property because he's the one who shot her."

He said Slade would be charged with carrying an unlicensed weapon, reckless use of a firearm, and inhumane treatment of animals. Once they'd checked on that box of credit cards, there might be other charges, too.

His partner got Slade to his feet.

"This guy's going to jail," he said.

When they passed close to the Bradens, Slade stopped. He fixed his angry gaze on James.

"You haven't seen the last of me," he said. "You owe me. Sooner or later, I'm going to collect."

James stared back at him. "I don't owe you anything. This was all your fault and you know it."

Slade lunged forward, but the officers restrained him.

"Enough of that," Officer Ryan said. "Let's go."

Then he and his partner marched their prisoner up the hill. Slade kept trying to twist free of their grasp and repeatedly shouted, "You owe me!"

James did not reply. He just watched until Slade had disappeared from view.

The McAfees left soon after. Barry kept looking back over his shoulder, and James felt sure he wanted to stay and ask questions. His father's firm grip on his arm urged Barry back to their car instead.

Finally, only James and his family remained. He looked at his parents.

"Can we go home now?" he asked.

"Let's do that," his mother said.

Together, they all walked up the hill. James paused at the top for one more look back at the hollow. Already, the grass had begun to spring up again, and a scattering of wildflowers were opening their petals to the late-day sun. It had regained its aura of mystery.

He smiled. Z'Nia would have been pleased.

Then he turned and followed his family to the car.

CHAPTER 35

James

The Bradens' house had a small back porch, just a couple of concrete steps leading down into the yard. James sat on the bottom one. Towering oaks, a few maples, and a couple of tall evergreens encircled the lawn, turning it into a private space. Here, he could be alone. Here, he could think.

He wondered, *Why has nothing changed?*

Little more than six hours ago, he'd been in the cave behind the waterfall. He thought what had happened there was a world-changing event. And yet, life still went on as before. The earth had not stopped rotating on its axis or fallen from its orbit. Minutes still rolled into hours, the hours into days, and the autumn days into approaching winter. Didn't the earth know its protector was gone?

Above him, the last of the afternoon's storm clouds blew off to the east. The moon slid into view, pale against the darkening sky. As he watched, the first stars came out, tempting James to make a wish.

I'm too old for that, he thought. He didn't believe in wishes any more. Not after today.

All around him, brittle oak leaves whispered like pages in an old book—*hushhh*. As if attracted by the sound, a crow settled on a low branch. James had rarely seen a bird flying so late in the day. He wondered if this might be the one he'd seen earlier near the waterfall. Could it have followed him home?

"Was it you?" James asked.

The bird cocked its head. Its eyes glittered in the light cast by the porch fixture.

"Won't talk, huh? Guess I'll never know."

But after all the improbable things that had happened that day, he decided this must be the same bird.

"Thanks for trying to help," he said, and the crow's head bobbed as if in reply.

A gust of wind ruffled James's hair. He turned up his jacket collar and slid his hands into flannel-lined pockets. He shifted his weight, trying to ease his sore muscles. The cement step felt cold and hard, and the temperature was nearing the freezing mark, but he wasn't ready to go back inside yet.

Ever since he'd met Josh in the forest that afternoon, James had been surrounded by people. His family. The McAfees. The police. Mom had even insisted on visiting the emergency room to have his injuries checked. The hospital had been noisy and crowded. When he'd been pronounced okay, James was glad to leave.

At dinner time, he couldn't bring himself to eat. After pushing the food around his plate for several minutes, he'd excused himself to go outside. He'd needed to get away from everyone, away from the stares they tried not to let him see and the questions they wouldn't ask.

They all want to know what happened, he thought.

He didn't blame them. He planned to tell his family eventually. He'd tell Matt, too. They deserved to know the truth, or at least some of it.

But not tonight.

Tonight he needed to think about all the amazing and terrible events of the past few days. He had to try to make sense of it all and decide how much information he could share.

James knew he'd have to tell his family something. Otherwise, his parents would start worrying and Lindsey might begin watching him again. Even Matt would wonder why he was being so secretive.

I'll tell them as much as I can, James thought. *Just not everything.*

Like Z'Nia's healing powers, for example. Nobody needed to know about that. Who'd believe it anyway? Everyone would think he'd imagined it. Josh would probably start teasing him about his brain being affected by the bump on his head. No, his story was incredible enough without that detail.

For the same reason, he would never tell anyone about having a mind-link with Z'Nia. Even his family would think that was strange. He knew it would make them uncomfortable. They'd all start looking at him sideways, wondering if he could read their minds. They might start guarding their thoughts, just in case. Maybe they'd avoid spending time with him.

And that would be awful, he thought.

James couldn't tell anyone about the cave behind the waterfall either. He owed it to Z'Nia to keep that to himself. Though he trusted his family and his best friend, he knew any of them might let something slip without meaning to. And that could send crowds of curiosity seekers into the woods to look for her remains. He wouldn't let that happen, not if he could help it.

Finally, he would never let any of them know what he'd done in the cave that day. They wouldn't understand about him saying death prayers over a creature they could only regard as a "dumb animal." Even Matt, who had seen Z'Nia and knew she was special, would have a hard time believing it. James could hardly believe it himself.

His thoughts were interrupted by a warm nudge against his elbow. He looked down to see Shadow standing next to him.

"Hey, boy," James said. "Who let you out?"

He rubbed his hand across that warm black head and realized the dog held a ball in his mouth. Shadow looked at James expectantly.

James took the ball and bounced it into the yard. It rolled outside the pool of light that surrounded the porch. Shadow ran off. A minute later, the collie emerged from the darkness, once more carrying the ball. James saw he was limping and remembered Shadow was nearly ten years old.

"You love to play fetch, don't you?" James asked. He took the ball and pulled his arm back for another throw.

Then he heard a voice in his head, a voice from long ago.

Animals are not toys, it said.

When he'd first heard Z'Nia say those words, he hadn't understood what she meant. Now he did.

He let his arm fall into his lap. "Sorry. You don't have to do any tricks tonight, Shadow. Never again, unless you want to. Let's just sit here, okay?"

Shadow turned in a circle a couple of times and then lay down at the base of the steps, his chin resting on James's foot.

"Nothing's going to be the same ever again, is it, boy?" James asked.

In his mind, he could almost hear the dog answering, *No, James, it isn't.*

James smiled. "Glad we agree on that."

Then, deciding it might help to put his thoughts into words, he pretended Shadow could really understand him, and he continued the conversation.

"Everything's so confusing. I thought I knew the difference between right and wrong. Like, it's wrong to steal, isn't it? But I had to help Z'Nia even if Slade did think I was stealing from him. I didn't have much of a choice, did I?"

Shadow blinked at him.

No choice at all, he seemed to say. *You did what you had to do.*

"That's what I thought, too. So saving her life was more important. But that brings up another question. Whose life is worth the most anyway? Mine? Z'Nia tried to protect me from Slade, and she cleared all those vines away even though she was wounded."

James imagined Shadow's answer. *That's her way.*

"Yeah, you're right," James said. "It's what they do. The Tazsmin, I mean. But, see, that made her about the most important creature on the face of the planet, didn't it? She was a healer, and they're pretty rare. Shouldn't she have put herself first? Shouldn't I have been the one to save her?"

The dog tilted its head to one side as if considering how to answer. *You tried.*

"I know I tried," James said. "But it wasn't enough. I don't understand how I could try so hard and still fail. She had an amazing gift. Why should she be the one to die? And why couldn't I do more to save her? All I did was say some words to make her feel better. I couldn't even remember the right thing to say. It's kind of like the bad guys won."

Shadow looked up at him, his deep brown eyes like pools of wisdom. *She's free. Isn't that what you wanted?*

"Yeah, but not like this."

James shook his head. "I feel like it was all my fault. I wanted to help her, so I insisted she get on the truck. And I'm the one who kicked over that box. If I hadn't done that, Slade might have been willing to let us go. Z'Nia might still be alive."

Maybe, the dog seemed to say. *And maybe not. But either way, you did your best. Sometimes that's all you can do.*

James sighed. "Yeah, I guess."

Then he remembered Z'Nia telling him much the same thing that afternoon. He ran his hand over the dog's coat.

"You're pretty smart, you know that?"

His fingers found a thorn, buried deep in Shadow's fur. The dog whined softly as James pulled it out.

"Does that hurt, boy? I'm sorry."

167

James rubbed gently at the spot. Into his mind came a vision of Z'Nia healing the sparrow. In honor of her memory, he repeated her song as well.

"Grow in love. Grow in peace," he whispered. The words hung in the air like the breath of the wind.

James felt the dog's pulse beating warm beneath his fingertips. They sat motionless for the space of a few beats. Then Shadow licked his face.

"You're welcome, boy," James said.

He got to his feet. He was ready to be with other people again. Maybe he'd even answer a few of their questions.

As if it didn't want to be alone, the crow left its perch and flew away to the north. Its melancholy cry pierced the air. James looked after it, but the darkness had swallowed it up.

"Come on, Shadow," he said. "It's been a long day. Let's go inside and get warm."

He held the door so the dog could go first. Shadow bounded into the house like a puppy, no longer limping at all.

ॐ   ॐ   ॐ

Z'Nia

Miles away, in the cave behind the waterfall, Z'Nia felt the dog's injury vanish. James had healed it, though he probably didn't know that.

The fire James had built hours earlier now burned brightly once again. Light flickered across her paintings: sun … tree … bird … deer … and one of herself holding the hand of a small boy. The light flickered, too, across a new painting that showed an older boy, the one Z'Nia trusted above all living beings. She had begun working on it that very day.

She had awakened hours earlier, surprised to find herself lying on the floor of the cave, her face covered with a blanket. She'd pushed it back and looked around.

I am home, she'd realized.

The last thing she remembered was hearing the wind call her name as the blackness closed in around her. When it stopped, she must have gone to sleep.

Now she sighed. *And when I awoke, James was gone.*

And so was the pain, she reminded herself.

She stroked more pigment onto her painting, careful of the shoulder that still felt a bit stiff.

I may never see him again, she thought. *He thinks I am dead.*

She felt sad, but her sorrow was mingled with joy. She would always have her memories of James. And though she might not see him, she knew she would never be truly alone again.

Today, in this cave, something unexpected had happened. The song that had been meant to heal her spirit had healed her injured body as well. James had brought her back from the very brink of death. She did not know why or how it had happened. She knew only that she was alive, though her injuries should have been fatal.

She worried a little about James. The healing power could be a heavy responsibility, even for a Tazsmin. Though unsure how it would affect a human, she hoped it would bring him satisfaction. She hoped it would bring him happiness.

Years may pass before James fully understands the power he has been given, she thought. *He will have no one to teach him, but I believe he will use it well. It is a great gift.*

Z'Nia dabbed on a final stroke of pigment.

There, she said to herself. *Finished.*

She stepped back to admire the painting, knowing it would help her remember this day.

I have good reason to celebrate, she thought, *not because I survived, but because the earth has found another healer to help with my work.*

It had been a long time since Z'Nia had talked to her mother. In all her years of captivity, she had felt alone. Now, here in their familiar cave, she felt Mother's presence once again, and she welcomed it. It seemed natural to share her news.

Can you believe it, Mother? she asked. *A human has saved the life of a Tazsmin. Who would have imagined such an amazing thing could happen? Who would ever have believed that a human could become the next WindSinger?*

169

CPSIA information can be obtained
at www.ICGtesting.com
Printed in the USA
LVOW12s1903080418
572690LV00004B/415/P